Like A Dead Man Walking

And Other Shadow Tales

By

William F. Nolan

Edited, with a Biographical Introduction, by Jason V Brock

Dark Regions Press
– 2018 –

Edited by Jason V Brock
Cover Art by David Ho
Cover + Interior Design by Cyrus Wraith Walker

Dark Regions Press, LLC.
500 Westover Drive #12565
Sanford, NC 27330
United States of America

www.darkregions.com

Second Trade Paperback Edition
ISBN-10: 1-72580-256-2
ISBN-13: 978-1-72580-256-8

ACKNOWLEDGEMENTS

"Introduction: The Inner World of William F. Nolan" Copyright © 2013 by Jason V Brock. New to this collection.

"The Blood Countess" Copyright © 2013 by William F. Nolan and Jason V Brock. New to this collection.

"Dread Voyage" Copyright © 2011 by William F. Nolan. First printed in *The Devil's Coattails: More Dispatches from the Dark Frontier* (Cycatrix Press, 2011). Previously uncollected.

"Flight to Legend" Copyright © 2013 by William F. Nolan. New to this collection.

"Getting Along Just Fine" Copyright © 2010 by William F. Nolan. First printed in *The Bleeding Edge: Dark Barriers, Dark Frontiers* (Cycatrix Press, 2009). Previously uncollected.

"Exchange" Copyright © 2013 by Jason V Brock and William F. Nolan. New to this collection.

"My Girl Name is Elly" Copyright © 2013 by William F. Nolan. New to this collection.

"The Recluse" Copyright © 2013 by William F. Nolan. New to this collection.

"Dysfunctional" Copyright © 2013 by William F. Nolan. New to this collection.

"Descent" Copyright © 2010 by William F. Nolan. First published in *Calliope* magazine.

"Ashland" Copyright © 2013 by William F. Nolan. Version new to this collection.

"Millikin's Machine" Copyright © 2013 by William F. Nolan. New to this collection.

"The End: A Final Dialogue" Copyright © 2013 by William F. Nolan. New to this collection.

"The Beach" Copyright © 2013 by Jason V Brock and William F. Nolan. New to this collection.

"With the Dark Guy" Copyright © 2015 by William F. Nolan. New to the second edition of the collection.

AUTHOR'S PREFACE

*Like a Dead Man Walking is my thirty-first collection. Most of these have featured short fiction, but a few contain non-fiction or verse, and one (*Ill Met by Moonlight*) gathers together a selection of my best artwork. This current volume collects mostly never-before-printed material, with a limited number of special reprints. Moving toward my 88th year, I continue to write, but plan to retire on my 100th birthday (of course I expect to reach it). In our fact-oriented computer age, short magazine fiction is, sad to say, nearly extinct—but book publishers continue to keep me going with fresh collections of my work. God bless 'em! Long may they prosper!*

—WFN

William F. Nolan
I owe profound thanks to Jason & Sunni Brock for their tireless work on this collection. Jason helped shape the final contents, made valued corrections and additions to many of the new stories, and was my able collaborator on several of them. His wife, Sunni, also functioned as a "silent" co-editor, providing key plot and character contributions. This book would not exist without them.

Finally, I wish to thank everyone at Dark Regions Press. The road has been a long one, but the journey has been well worthwhile.

—WFN

Jason V Brock
I would like to thank my wife, Sunni, for her support and encouragement, as well as everyone at Dark Regions Press. Also, I'd like to tip my hat to William F. Nolan for putting up with my *relentless* badgering to get the book done and in good shape.

—JVB

Contents

Tributes

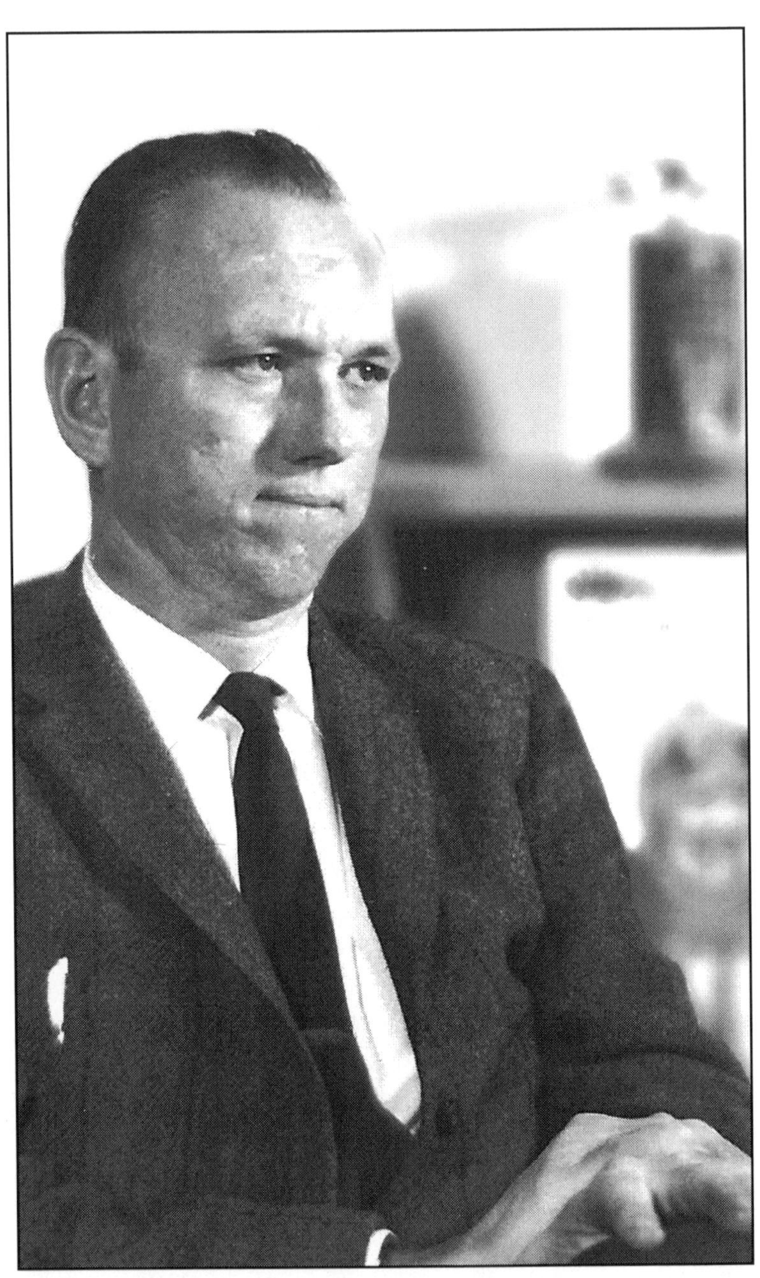

Nolan in the 1960s. (Courtesy William F. Nolan.)

Introduction: The Inner World of William F. Nolan

Note: When this book was going to be issued by the venerable Arkham House, I was asked by Nolan and the publisher not only to function as editor, but also to write the introduction. I was pleased to oblige. In the interval between the conception and the execution of this fine collection of stories, however, a bit of bad luck befell Arkham just as we were ready to go to press on the volume (in other words, it was completed, but the untimely passing of April Derleth was an unhappy conclusion to the nascent rebirth of that respected imprint).

Thankfully, Jerad Walters (he of the outstanding house Centipede Press) swooped in to the rescue and has, at last, produced the book, for which William F. Nolan and I are very grateful. The Centipede book sold out, which is why we are thankful now to Chris Morey and his team at Dark Regions Press, another fine publisher, for getting this slightly updated edition out in paperback.

William F. Nolan.

How does one approach the output of such a diverse and prolific author? Indeed, it is a daunting question, and not an easy one to answer. Therefore, to gather a true sense of the work, it is illuminating to contemplate the person responsible for it...

Who William F. Nolan *is*: Successful Hollywood screenwriter... Race car enthusiast... Fan of Ernest Hemingway...

Who William F. Nolan is *not*: A great writer (by his own estimation, Nolan claims that he is "a talented, even very good, stylist, but not a Faulkner or Mailer")... A person who easily cultivates deep relationships (Nolan again: "I have always been a bit too guarded and afraid to open up emotionally; I often use humor as a shield to keep others at a distance. It's one of my biggest regrets on a personal level.") … An easy person to grasp ("I'll always have a side that no one will know. Though I detest labels, I must confess that I'm a walking paradox! I lean toward mind-numbing preoccupations with numbers and routine, even as I recognize that I must remain open to change, or be left behind in today's world … I yearn for the imagined golden era of my youth, but realize that the patina of nostalgia is likely clouding my actual experiences … I'm politically liberal, but personally conservative … I feel for the underdog, but have a deep fascination with mean-spirited macho types like Hemingway, Steve McQueen and Frank Sinatra.") …

And, finally, who William F. Nolan *is*: An elder statesman of the classic science fiction and horror genres of the 1950s and '60s … A recognized expert on the pulp era, particularly the works of Dashiell Hammett and Max Brand … Close friend to the departed Richard Matheson (*I Am Legend, Bid Time Return*), the late Ray Bradbury (*Dark Carnival, The Martian Chronicles*), and the deceased Norman Corwin (*Norman Corwin Presents, Poet Laureate of Radio*).

Nolan, like most people, is a bundle of contradictions and cascading, amorphous mental impulses. He has gone through many changes in his eighty-plus years— such as reforming his once-overt chauvinism and embracing the feminine mystique, as well as ditching his speciesist inattention in favor of becoming an ardent vegetarian/animal-rights adherent—especially in the past decade. During this time, he has undergone a powerful interval of introspection, which has brought about a sort of inner revolution.

"A few years ago, when I relocated from Los Angeles—where I'd lived and worked for over 50 years—to Bend, Oregon, I had a bit of an existential crisis … I'd never been on my own before that, relocating as I did with my parents from Kansas City, Missouri, to San Diego when I was a teenager, and living with them until I married my wife, Cam. We were going through a rough time... It was the culmination of a long, slow-motion collision involving personal finances and other things—we had been together over thirty years by the time this was going on. So I moved away to do research for a book I was working on about Frederick Faust—better known as the productive Western writer Max Brand. It was quite a shock... The whole trauma of moving to a new part of the country, the resolution of the financial pressures, the uncertainty of our marital situation... All of that, plus Bend was like some other planet; I'm a city slicker—the outdoors is not my thing."

It was during this residence/exile in Bend that Nolan began to reassess his career... and what this mental construct of "William F. Nolan" really was: "My wife once said that I should realize that I am more than just the sum total of the books I've done or been in. She said that I needed to learn who *I* really am. At first I didn't understand what she meant, but the more time I spent alone, thinking about where I've been, what I've done, what I want to do, the more I came to understand the wisdom of her words. I *am*more than some books on the shelf, the lists that I make... My friends call me 'Bill'; 'William F. Nolan' is this other creature. He's sort of a benign alien persona... But I have to watch him—he can get the better of my best intentions with his tendency to overstate his importance and be impatient... That duality has hurt me at times in my career and helped me at others."

Though a successful screen and television writer for more than thirty years, he mostly stuck to projects that were "sure things" out of a fear of straying too far afield in the wilds of Hollywood (the majority of his output was for the dynamic producer/director Dan Curtis [*Dark Shadows, The Winds of War*]). In addition to being one of Curtis's go-to scribes, along with longtime friend Matheson—where he amassed credits such as *Trilogy of Terror, Burnt Offerings,* and *The Norliss Tapes*—Nolan is perhaps best known for his influential dystopian science-fiction masterpiece *Logan's Run* (which he co-authored with his friend George Clayton Johnson [*Ocean's 11, The Twilight Zone*]). Nolan later went on to write two sequels by himself—*Logan's Search* and *Logan's World* (and an as-yet unpublished follow-up called *Logan's Journey* with writer Paul McComas)—as well as act as a consultant for the eponymous 1976 MGM film and the short-lived TV series. During this era, he penned treatments of Peter Straub's *Floating Dragon* (unproduced), and an early iteration of what eventually became John Carpenter's bleak epic *The Thing* (based on John W. Campbell, Jr.'s seminal classic "Who Goes There?").

By his count, Nolan has produced more than 2000 pieces of writing. From profiles for magazines like *Playboy, Sports Illustrated,* and *Rogue* to short fiction (his omnibus horror collection, *Dark Universe,* was a finalist for the World Fantasy Award), novels, bibliographies (notably on personal friends and authors such as the late Messrs. Charles Beaumont [*The Hunger and Other Stories, The Intruder*], and Ray Bradbury [Nolan did *Ray Bradbury Review* early in his career, and later *The Ray Bradbury Companion*]), and several full-on biographies, including books on John Huston, McQueen, and Hammett.

Along the way, Nolan has found the time not only to speak at conventions, lecture and teach writing in college, but also to mentor younger writers, such as Dennis Etchison (*The Dark Country, California Gothic*), Joe R. Lansdale (*Vanilla Ride, The Bottoms*), and others. He has paid his dues to be sure, but on one wintry afternoon in Bend, Nolan found himself at a personal crossroads that no number of awards, no amount of praise, and no financial remuneration could resolve: What was he going to do with his life *now*?

"It was a tough time," he recalls. "I was sort of lost in Bend. I was on my own, in a new place. I hated the weather... But I knew that I couldn't go back to L.A. There was nothing there for me anymore. Hollywood was done with me as a screenwriter. I was lucky—I wrote scripts into my sixties; these days you're old if you're past forty! They just don't hire eighty-year-old screenwriters. They claim older folks are out of the loop with what young people are interested in seeing. So, as a result of moving away, I lost touch with many of my friends; in some cases, they had died. I had no living relatives... And the place [Los Angeles] had changed. It was not the same as when I was writing for Dan Curtis, or racing cars with John Tomerlin (*Challenge the Wind, The Fledgling*) and Beaumont... But it wasn't just that the place had changed. *I* had as well."

There were many pleas to return, from old friends like Bradbury and Etchison (even from his estranged wife), but Nolan felt that it was time he started a new chapter; that he *needed* to start one. He just wasn't sure what the story was—yet.

"After a yearandahalf or so, things began to thaw. I got involved with a documentary on my old pal Chuck Beaumont (*Charles Beaumont: The Short Life of Twilight Zone's Magic Man*), and that was what I needed to reconnect with the people I had lost contact with—George Johnson, Matheson, Frank M. Robinson (*The Power, The Glass Inferno*), Tomerlin and so on... It allowed me, ironically, to let go of the past in a way I had never been able to do previously; I became more open to the possibilities of the future... Consequently, I stopped feeling that my best days were behind me, that I was being passed by in the computer age, forgotten. Things started to fall into place even more when I moved to Vancouver."

The Vancouver he refers to is not in Canada: It is Vancouver, Washington, near Portland, OR. Once relocated from Bend to Vancouver to be closer to friends he had made during the production of the Beaumont documentary, Nolan hit his stride. "This is the most productive I've been since the 1950s." Lofty praise: the '50s was when he was one of the key players in that storied Southern California writing collective—known simply as "The Group" by insiders—which included Beaumont, Matheson, Johnson, Tomerlin, Bradbury, and others (by extension even Rod Serling, Theodore Sturgeon [*More Than Human, Not Without Sorcery*], Robert Bloch [*Strange Eons, Psycho*], and, toward the end of their confederation, a young Harlan Ellison[*Deathbird Stories, Dangerous Visions*]). This was the core braintrust of what is now considered classic science fiction and horror in literature and television for the modern and postmodern age; their influence has been pervasive and profound, and is the foundation of contemporary sensibilities regarding what Dark Fantasy and S/F are capable of achieving.

This frantic period with The Group was also a time when Nolan was still involved in the art world, before he decided to become a full-fledged author (he is an able draughtsman, and once had his own art studio in San Diego). The transition to writer came after he met Charles Beaumont. Nolan: "Chuck was the one that helped me become the person that I am today—I was still a hick from Kansas City, and he introduced me to literature and music, like Trumbo, Steinbeck, Fitzgerald, Mozart, and Ravel. We even raced cars together, as I mentioned. He was an incredible influence on me, on *all* of us... I think of him like a comet streaking through the sky. We were best friends for ten years; I still miss him."

Beaumont was a tragic figure: The main writer for *The*

Twilight Zone after Serling, he was also a top author for *Playboy* and a budding screenwriter for Otto Preminger (he was contracted for an unproduced treatment of *Bunny Lake is Missing*), George Pal (*The Wonderful World of the Brothers Grimm, The Seven Faces of Dr. Lao*), and Roger Corman, including *Night of the Eagle,* and *The Intruder.* This latter film was based on his novel of the same name—Beaumont, along with Nolan, Johnson, and Robinson, starred in the picture, alongside a brilliant William Shatner. Beaumont died in 1967 at the age of thirty-eight from a mysterious disease that manifested itself as a form of pre-senile dementia accompanied with premature aging. His death would be a devastating event for his family (he left a wife and four young children), as well as The Group. Over the years, Group members would all slowly drift apart without Beaumont as the nucleus. "Chuck was the hub, the core," Nolan reflects. "Without him, we separated and went our own ways... I hadn't realized how much I missed all the rest of The Group until Brock's documentary sort of reunited us all."

Even though he has made a living as a professional writer for over half a century—with numerous awards, roughly twenty produced scripts and over eighty books to his credit—he's not content to retire just yet. "Right now I'm working on several books (among them a new Logan novel, *Logan Falls*), a horror comic (*Tales from William F. Nolan's Dark Universe*) *and* I write for the print magazine *[NameL3ss].* I'm also active on social media (Facebook and Twitter), and have a website (www.WilliamFNolan.com). I attend cons throughout the year, such as World Fantasy and the World Horror Convention. There's a big-budget remake of *Logan's Run* in pre-production from Warner's, too."

This creator of Logan, a world authority on pulpmeister Max Brand and The Black Mask Boys, the editor of nearly thirty anthologies and a figure lauded by the likes of Stephen King, Rod Serling, and Dean Koontz, presses forward on all fronts—as a genre-defying author, poet, and artist; in all media (print, online, film); and in his outreach to others (as a mentor to young writers, a spokesperson for animals, and a conscientious friend). Nolan seems at a third personal and creative peak (the first being the 1950s–early'60s; the second in the 1970s–early '80s), and is as sharp, witty, and outgoing as ever. Part of the reason for this particular revival is the newfound sense of his previous accomplishments—and his realistic appraisal of his place in the cosmology of literature and the human drama.

"I used to work at cross-purposes," he says. "I would toetheline for things that were not true to the *real,* innerWilliam F. Nolan. I would deny things to myself even though I knew they were right. For example, I was raised as a Catholic. Years later, Beaumont and I were doing something, and he looked at me and said 'You will eventually leave the Church.' I was stunned! And I adamantly denied it ... Later, after Chuck died, I did leave it, though. I now think that the Church warped my mother's faith and poisoned me in certain ways ... I consider myself an 'Anti-Catholic'."

In spite of his stern feelings regarding "Organized Religion as a crutch," Nolan does maintain a strong belief in the spiritual—and supernatural—realm. "I believe in reincarnation. I also think that ghosts are real. I mean, it's silly to think that everyone becomes one, but I do think that there is such a thing as a ghost ... There are many things that we don't understand in the universe, but that doesn't mean that they don't exist. I think zombies and werewolves and such are ridiculous. And the zodiac is silly, too. Of course, aliens are real ... "

He has also matured in his view of his parents. "My

father, Mike Nolan, was not an intellectual, but he was an adventurous man. He drove the first car along the Santa Fe Trail into New Mexico and even joined the hunt with 'Black Jack' Pershing for Pancho Villa in Mexico ... I was the opposite type of personality, but he loved me in spite of it! He liked the fact that I was an avid reader, an artist, and writer. He took pride in that.

"Of course, I adored my mother, Bernadette. I was a real 'Mother's Boy.' She was the reason I stayed with the Church as long as I did, out of deference to her. They were both pure Irish ... I'm 100% Irish. Sadly, I've come to realize that my parents were human, just like everyone else.

"Growing up, I thought they were perfect, but I see now that they were good people, and I loved them dearly, but they were flawed. They were both functional alcoholics. I feel that my own issues with forming deep, close bonds stems from the lack of boundaries I had growing up ... I was allowed to do *anything*, even if it was not good for me. If I didn't want to study something in school, they wouldn't force me to. If I wanted to eat just sugar and not do chores, that was OK with them ... In retrospect, I should have had more discipline as a child. I think that it would have helped me in my later relations with people, especially with females."

Nolan's contemplation about his upbringing is tempered by his thoughts regarding the future, and his aspirations. Like most people, he has certain goals that he has yet to fulfill, and fears that keep him awake. "I hope that my best work will be remembered—and not just *Logan's Run*. *Logan* has been both a blessing and a curse. No one knows *me* if they see me walking down the street, but most folks know that book. They aren't aware that I've done other ones! I would like to have other works that transcend *Logan.* I think that's natural for any creator. It's not even my best book! I feel that *The Marble*

Orchard is my best book. I want to achieve real status as a quality writer, and not just for my genre works, though I am proud of what I've done.

"I *do* worry about falling behind. Joe R. Lansdale once said that to me 'Whatever you do, don't fall behind!' Joe was right. I have no children, and I have insecurities about my place, so I feel I've got to keep active... I have a need to get out there. I enjoy my fans, and relish quality time with my friends. No one knows what tomorrow may hold, and I've had a great run by anyone's estimation, but I still feel that I have a lot to get done. I have more to say. I just have to have the wherewithal to get it out there. History will be the final judge. All any of us can do is to try, and hope that we can connect with all the other folks out there like us... In that respect I've been a lucky man indeed."

As William F. Nolan closes in on his 90th journey around the sun, he feels more than ever that the future is bright...

And as dark as he wants it to be.

Jason V Brock

William F. Nolan today

Elizabeth Bathory: a woman who bathed in virgin's blood. Her madness is a rich substrate for horror. Are vampires real or imagined? Can they possibly be frightening in the modern era? Read this and decide…

—WFN/JVB

THE BLOOD COUNTESS

"Once the trained planarian flatworms learn to negotiate the labyrinth, they are ground up and fed to a group of untrained worms, who then assimilate the knowledge of how to negotiate the maze." Professor Ted Donner allows the statement to hang in the air. Noting the rising level of disgust on his students' faces, he proceeds. "I know, horrible isn't it? Regardless, it would appear, simply from having digested their trained compatriots, that we have reinforced our original hypothesis—that certain characteristics can be *physically* transferred from being to being." The Professor pauses again, then: "In other words, some behaviors are passed along a genetic pathway that bypasses the more well-known mechanisms of learning: research, the aggregation of knowledge, imitation, cogitation, and so on . . ."

A female student stands up in the back row. "Are we then to assume, Professor Donner, that the path to prior knowledge lies in cannibalism?"

A ripple of laughter from her classmates.

A woman enters the room as Donner replies: "We are human beings, Miss Brook, not flatworms. I seriously doubt that by devouring, say, Michelangelo, that I would then acquire his skills in painting or sculpture. Now, if you'll—" The end-of-class buzzer cuts short his sentence.

As the students file out, Donner reminds them: "You all have tomorrow's assignment… and remember, on Friday, we have our mid-term exam. Be warned!"

This elicits a groan from the departing students.

Donner is scribbling a note at his desk as the woman approaches. "Hello, Ted."

He looks up, breaks into a wide smile. "Joan Maitland! My lord, it's been—"

"Almost five years."

He takes her hand. "Great to see you! What about Dave. Is he here with you?"

She shakes her head. "No, Dave's still at Warwick House." She hesitates, an intensity in her sad brown eyes. "Can we talk somewhere? It's important."

"Of course. How about lunch at Banducci's? Still go for Italian?"

"It doesn't matter," she says.

"It'll be just like old times."

Her smile is wan. "Right, Ted… just like old times."

The restaurant is small, crowded, rustically Italian in decor. Most of the patrons are University students, happy and boisterous. Donner and Joan take a booth in the rear, ordering wine, a caprese salad and manicotti.

"Really good seeing you again," he says. "When we… Well, I took it pretty hard."

"I never meant to hurt you." She takes his hand. "I still care for you, Ted. I hated breaking off our engagement, but Dave and I—"

"You don't have to explain," he says. "I admit I was hurt when you left, but I'm a big boy; I got through it. I just wanted you to be happy, and Dave filled the bill, it seems."

"Well, I *was* happy." Her voice trails off.

"But you're not now?"

"No, not now."

Ted is intrigued. "Tell me about it."

"We've separated."

He frowns. "Never thought it could happen. You seemed perfect for each other."

She looks down, twisting the linen napkin in her lap. "I didn't want to leave him, but he forced me to go. *Demanded* I leave. It's the house … it's changed him."

"I don't get it," Ted replies. He takes a sip of wine. "How could a house cause you and Dave to break up?"

She looks up at him, her voice strained. "Do you believe that … that a house can be *evil*, that it can project a … a kind of spell over those who—"

"C'mon, Joan! No house is good *or* evil—just a pile of wood and stones, nothing more."

Her tone is impassioned. "You're *wrong!* This is Warwick House … It has a terrible history. We never should have bought it. I never felt safe there."

"You say it changed Dave … How? How did it change him?"

She pauses, looking into the distance. "For one thing, he refuses to talk about his new book. When I asked him about it, he became withdrawn, short-tempered. We began having violent arguments … He made it clear that he no longer wanted me there. So I finally left."

Donner leans back in the booth, turning the wine glass on the table. "When did all this happen?"

"Three months ago."

"Have you been in contact since then?"

Their salad arrives. She picks at the food, unable to eat. "I haven't heard a word from him in the past three months.

I even tried writing to him, but he never answered."

"Have you called him?"

"No phones at Warwick. Dave ripped them out of the wall."

She leans across the table. "I came to you because I don't know who else to turn to."

Ted is confused. "But what do you want me to do? I'm a University professor, not a marriage counselor. I don't know what I'd be able to—"

Her eyes blaze with emotion. "You could *see* him, *talk* to him. I have to know where I stand in his life. Does he want a divorce? Is our marriage over?"

"And I'm supposed to find out?"

She sighs deeply. "I don't know anyone else to ask."

"Been a long time since Dave and I were close. When you came along... The point is, we're no longer close. I'm not sure he'll even talk to me."

She regards him, eyes glinting. "Dave has always spoken warmly of you... of the old days. I believe that you're the only one he *will* talk to."

A moment of silence between them. "Obviously you still love him."

She nods, head down. "Yes, I do. I still love him."

"All right," Ted declares, "I have some vacation time due. I'll get a fill-in for my classes and drive up to see Dave."

"When?"

He looks into her eyes. "This weekend. Okay?"

A relieved smile brightens her face. "I really appreciate your help." She touches his arm.

His voice is tinged with humor. "I just hope that Warwick House likes me!"

Later that evening, Eli Clark, white-haired and stooped, limps across the parking area behind the University. The school is banded on three sides by neatly-trimmed grass lawns with the concrete parking area in the rear. Now only one car is parked there, a dusty orange station wagon. Carrying a long-handled broom, tin bucket, and a bag of cleaning materials, Clark unlocks a side door and enters the main building. As he dumps his cleaning equipment in the lower hall, he notices a light burning behind frosted glass at the far end of the hallway. The school library. Clark taps on the door, then opens it.

A dark-haired young teacher, Peggy Ames, is working at a reference table, making notes on a stack of papers.

"Saw the station wagon out back. Figured it was you. I gotta clean up in here pronto. How late you 'spect to work tonight?"

"I just have to finish grading these tests. Be done soon. Fifteen . . . twenty minutes at most."

"Okie-doke, I'll be on the stairs scrubbin' 'em down. Won't be no bother to you."

She smiles and goes back to work.

Minutes tick by on the library wall clock. A *thudding* sound from the stairway.

Peggy gets up from her papers and moves out into the hall. Opening the stairway door, she peers upward. "Mr. Clark? Are you all right? I heard a noise."

A shadow flits across the stairs.

"Is that *you*, Mr. Clark?"

Silence.

Peggy begins climbing the stairs, reaches the second floor, and gasps. The old janitor is sprawled on the concrete dec;, his head is across the room, the white hair blood-matted. Crouching over his body like a vulture is a woman. She raises her bloody face toward Peggy, lips drawn back from rows of razor-sharp fangs . . .

"A woman … up there … she killed Mr. Clark!" Peggy's voice wavers in hysteria.

Deputies Fred Blanchard and Wayne Stoddard are in the lower hall, weapons in hand. "Stay here," says Blanchard, "while we check this out."

They head up the stairway.

The next day, Sheriff Jim Baxter, a thick-necked, wide-bodied man in his late fifties, leans forward over his desk, scowling at Deputy Stoddard's report. Blanchard, the younger deputy, tall, a bit overweight, in dark glasses, stands next to Stoddard, nervously biting his lip.

"And when we reached the second floor," says Stoddard, "there was poor old Clark, dead as all hell."

"And the mystery woman?" prompts Baxter.

"Gone. No trace of her."

"Check for prints?"

"None."

"Did you get a description from Ms. Ames?"

"Nope," replies Stoddard. "She's in shock. Won't say a word."

"Where is she now?"

"Park View Hospital. Under sedation."

Doctor Steven Kane, in ward whites, shakes his head, looking down at Peggy Ames in a raised hospital bed. Eyes glazed, she stares ahead, unmoving.

"She's just not responding, Sheriff," he says to Baxter.

"Is she still drugged?"

"No, the effects of the sedatives have worn off. That isn't the problem."

"Then what is?"

"Sometimes, when an individual undergoes a severe

emotional trauma, they check out mentally... Ms. Ames is in a state of shock. She's totally out of touch with the world around her."

"Which leaves us without a description of the woman who allegedly murdered Clark. Ames was the only one who saw the killer."

"I realize that, but—"

"How long before she comes out of this?"

"No way to tell," says Kane. "Her mind has rejected what she's seen. She could remain like this for a day... a week... a month."

"Is there any way to break through to her?"

"Sorry, Sheriff—but whatever Ames has seen is locked away in her mind. We can't reach her. We'll just have to wait."

Two nights later, a black-and-white patrol car is parked on the shoulder of the highway near Shannon Road. Inside, at the wheel, Deputy Fred Blanchard finishes writing up a traffic stop. The night is still, save for the sound of crickets from the thick woods on each side of the highway.

Blanchard exits the patrol car, stretches, yawns, and leans back against the fender, his face pale in the dim glow of his cigarette.

A figure watches him from the inked woods. Glides closer. Watching. Advancing. Closer. Very close now, coming up directly behind him.

A snapping twig alerts Blanchard. He swings around, eyes probing the night. Something moves toward him in the night. He tosses away the cigarette and fumbles with his holster, pulling out a .38 revolver. He brings the gun up, fires. One... two... three shots.

The dark figure does not flinch; instead it shrieks, descending on him, savaging him.

Warwick House: Donner stops the car in front of a large granite boulder with the letters "W. H." cut into it, marking the entrance to a narrow dirt road leading from the secondary two-lane highway into thick Connecticut woods.

A stone wall, which once separated the yard from the surrounding terrain is now a tumbled ruin. At the road's end, a rusted iron gate lies half-buried in weed-choked brush; beyond it, topping a darkly-forested hill, the looming bulk of the mansion.

Who would want to live out here in such a godforsakenplace? Donner muses. *House is a fucking wreck… And the grounds are right out of a Frederick Law Olmsted nightmare!*

He eases his car forward.

Heavy vines and branches slash at the closed windows as his car steadily climbs the hill, coming to a stop facing a wide Victorian porch. Broken steps lead up to the massive front door.

Ted exits the car, staring at the imposing façade. Warwick House still retains its faded grandeur: At the century's turn, such houses were built in the manner of castles, and this one is still noble. Yet, with age, the decaying mansion has taken on a menacing aura, its angles sharp, its architecture somehow extra-dimensional. The leaded-glass windows seem to stare back at Donner, defying him to enter.

Maybe Dave isn't here any longer. Place looks like a showcase for Horror Homes and Gardens… *Certainly no sign of life that I can detect…*

Donner mounts the porch, the weathered footboards groaning under his weight. The door is of heavy oak, and the pitted brass knocker is carved as a devil's head, tongue out, eyes protruding.

Ugly, damn ugly!

Ted snaps the heavy knocker against the wood: A

thudding drumbeat. No response. He tries again, and the tall oak door creaks inward. Donner pushes his way inside.

He peers into the evening gloom of the house. Silence and cobwebs. Dust-cloaked furniture. A pervading sense of rot and corruption.

No wonder this place gave Joan the creeps.

"Dave!" Loudly. "It's me, Ted Donner." A pause. "Do you hear me?"

His shout echoes through the cavernous abode, but there is no reply. Donner walks forward, down a musty, shadowed hallway leading to the main living room. He stops to gaze upward at a large oil painting hanging above the chipped-stone fireplace. It is a scene of despair and violence: several voluptuous nude women are apparently engaged in an orgy; their bodies—firm, ripe—are slicked in gore. The lone male figure in the image is reclining on a chaise lounge; his head has been removed, yet the women seem to be sexually defiling his body in spite of it.

Christ, that's hideous! Who would have such a thing on display?

Ted continues to check out the mansion as he walks through it: crystal chandeliers, their glitter long-since obscured in grime, massive carved antique tables, thick velvet drapes over high windows... with a wide stairway leading upward.

Maybe Dave's upstairs. Didn't hear me come in.

Ted climbs the stairs, avoiding gaps, wary of the rickety banister. He moves along another dim hallway draped in gray cobwebs. A closed door at the end of the hall draws his attention. He knocks.

"It's Ted Donner." He hesitates, then opens the door.

In the bedroom, Dave Maitland is sprawled face-down on a bare mattress. He's wearing a greasy pajama top and a ragged pair of sweat pants. Unshaven. No shoes.

Ted is shocked. He nudges Dave's shoulder. Maitland rolls over, sits up, blinking in the room's pale afternoon light.

He squints up at his friend. "Ted! For Christ's sake, how did you get here?"

"Walked in when no one answered the door. Wasn't even sure you were still in the house. You look lousy."

"Got a killer headache," says Maitland. He groans, shakes his head. "Need a drink."

They go downstairs. Dave leads Donner to the kitchen. A half-filled bottle of bourbon sits on the dining table.

Maitland tips the bottle to his lips, takes a long swallow. "Ugh! Good stuff." He offers the bottle to Donner. "Have a shot."

"I'll pass," says Donner.

Maitland sets the bottle back on the table and settles heavily into a chair. "Been a helluva long time since we hung out."

"It has," nods Ted.

Dave chuckles. "Remember when we were both courting Joan and you said 'May the best man win.' Remember that?"

"I remember. And you won."

Ted sits down at the table.

Maitland rubs a slow finger along his stubbled jaw. "Course I know why you're here."

"Figured you would."

"Joan thinks that by sending you—"

"... that you'll talk to me. About this whole sad situation."

"Worried, is she?"

"She's very upset. Asked me to see you. *Can* we talk?"

"Sure, we can—but first, I need another shot." Again, he tips up the bottle.

"Hitting that stuff pretty hard."

"That's my business," snaps Maitland. "What I drink is of no concern to you."

"Just an observation," Donner says.

Maitland eases back in his chair. "All right, Teddy boy, let's talk."

"Joan is very unhappy at the way things have gone between you," Ted says. "What the hell's happened to you, Dave… living out here all alone… rattling around this rotted old house… sleeping away the afternoons?"

Maitland shrugs. "I usually write after dark. That's why I was sleeping. Was up all night working on my book."

"What's it about?"

"Never mind what it's about." His tone is suddenly sharp.

"Okay, okay… I was just curious. Used to be, I could never shut you up when it came to telling me about your work."

"That was then. This is now."

"Forget I ever asked."

Maitland stares at his old friend. "I take it you don't much care for Warwick House."

"I find it… rather gloomy. What inspired you to buy it? Joan never liked old houses."

"It was my choice." He looks up, surveying the kitchen. "You know, this was a showplace at the turn of the century. Old Warwick put a fortune into this joint. The president himself stayed here in 1906."

"Granted, it's impressive. Or once was. But I still don't see you living in it."

"Neither could Joan."

"She says you asked her to leave… *demanded* it."

"That's true. Joan never tried to understand what this place means to me. Her growing hatred for Warwick House corrupted our relationship."

"She still loves you, Dave… but she's not sure if you still love her. *Do* you?"

Dave shrugs. “Doesn’t matter whether I do or not. It’s too late for us.”

“I don’t understand.”

“Don’t try. Just accept what I’m saying.”

“Joan won’t be pleased.”

Dave stands up from the table. “Perhaps you’d better go, Ted. It’s nearly dark, and the road to the highway is difficult to negotiate at night.”

Donner looks surprised. “But there’s more we need to talk about. Why can’t I stay over in one of the guest rooms?”

“No, that’s not possible.” Dave is nervous, his voice edged.

“But why not?”

“The rooms aren’t prepared. I have no facilities for guests.”

“Hell, Dave, I’m no ‘guest’. Don’t see why I can’t—”

Maitland cuts him off. “You’ll have to go. I insist.”

He walks Donner to the door, opens it. “I’m sorry, but this is how it has to be. Some things I just can’t let you in on. Goodbye Ted.”

Donner hesitates in the open doorway, confused by his old friend’s odd behavior. “Joan needs to see you, Dave. Maybe you should—”

A rush of words: “No, I can’t see her again. She must never come back here … never!”

Retreating into the house, the heavy oak door slamming behind Maitland, Donner draws in a deep breath, then moves toward his car. He climbs inside, starts the engine. Bumping along the dirt road, night has closed in and the passage is treacherous. Reaching the two-lane highway, he speeds up.

The dark figure of a woman suddenly appears in the middle of the road, starkly illumined by the headlights.

Donner brakes hard, his car skidding wildly. Stopping near the highway shoulder, he frantically looks behind him.

My God, did I hit her? I didn’t feel an impact…

The two-lane roadway is empty.

The woman is gone.

Later, Ted and Joan are in her Bridgehill apartment, seated in the sparsely-furnished living room. The apartment is small, purely functional. Unopened cartons fill one corner, and the walls are bare.

"I talked to Dave," he tells her, "but he doesn't want to see you." Donner pauses, reading the pain in her eyes. "He's not in good shape. He's a mess. And he's drinking too much. Hard liquor straight from the bottle."

"That doesn't surprise me," she says. "The heavy drinking started shortly after we moved into Warwick House."

"How much do you know about the book he's working on?"

"Very little. I know it's another historical … and that it has something to do with the seventeenth century."

"Dave used to talk a lot about his work."

"Yes, but that's all changed. Do you think what he's writing now has something to do with our breakup?"

"Possibly. There *could* be a connection." He leans toward her. "Tell me more about Warwick House."

"As I said, it has a strange history." She keeps her voice level, but Joan is obviously disturbed. "Hiram Warwick designed the place. Spared no expense. Wanted it to be the finest mansion in the state. It became an obsession with him. People say he was insane."

"Do you believe that?"

"He was certainly obsessed. And he died under mysterious circumstances. Same with his family. His first three children all died in their teens."

"What killed them?"

"No one knows. But it's really weird. I *do* know that

house is cursed. There's something not right about it."

Donner stood up, pacing the room. "Does Dave have any friends here in Bridgehill?"

"Just one. Jim Baxter, the sheriff. They used to hunt together. That was before we moved into Warwick House."

"Does Baxter know about Dave ... how he's changed?"

"Not really. He knows we split up, that I'm living alone here in town. Jim and I were never close. He's Dave's friend."

"I'll talk to him. He might have an angle on what's happened to Dave."

Joan nods. "It's worth a try."

Monday morning, Sheriff Jim Baxter stubs out his thin brown cigar in a glass ashtray on his desk. His office is a mass of stacked files, yellowed magazines, law books and bound case reports. Late afternoon sunlight creates shadow shapes in the cluttered room, as Baxter faces Ted Donner.

"Tell me about Dave Maitland."

"What's to tell? We were buddies. Still are, I guess. We've hunted together more than a few times. He's a pretty fair wing shot for a writer."

Donner is amused. "You're saying writers can't shoot straight?"

"They're not sporting types. Rather be hunched over a set of keys than freezing their ass off in a duck blind. But Dave's pretty good with a shotgun, like I said."

Donner frowns. "Me, I don't believe in shooting birds or any other living thing."

"To each his own," shrugs Baxter.

"Seen Dave lately?"

"Not since he moved into Warwick House."

"Don't you think it's a bit odd—splitting from his wife and shutting himself away in that house?"

Baxter shrugs again. "These things happen. Marriages go sour. People separate. As for his being in seclusion, hell, that's the way writers work. No big deal."

"Then you aren't worried about him?"

"Right now I'm worried about catching whoever killed Eli Clark—and just where my youngest deputy has got off to."

"Man of yours missing?"

"Yeah. Fred Blanchard. Hasn't called in. No sign of him or his black-and-white. Got an APB out."

"Could the two be connected?"

"What two?"

"Clark's death at the school and your deputy's disappearance."

"Dunno why they should be."

Ted stands, preparing to leave. "What do you know about Warwick House?"

"Just rumors. I hear old man Warwick was a real loony. You want to find out more about Warwick House . . . " He scribbles on a desk pad, hands the paper to Donner. " . . . here's the name of a guy who knows its history."

"Thanks. This might help clear up a few things."

Donner exits.

Ted is on the phone from his University office to Joan. Her voice is anxious. "Did you talk to Jim?"

"Just left there. He's not worried about Dave. Gave me a line about reclusive writers."

"So he was no help?"

"He supplied the name of a man to see at the Bridgehill Historical Society."

"I know the place. The old Victorian brick building on South Elm."

"Yep, that's it. Anyhow, the guy's name is Henstrom.

Local historian. I phoned him, said I was coming over, so we'll have to skip lunch."

"How about dinner instead?"

"You got it," says Donner.

"Ted, there's something else I was going to mention at lunch. Something I remembered about Dave's research."

"What about it?"

"When we first moved into Warwick, Dave left some papers on his desk. I just got a quick look at them before he locked everything away. Notes for his book, I think. I remember a one-word heading on several of them. The word was 'Bathory', B-A-T-H-O-R-Y. Does that mean anything to you?"

"No," Donner says, "but I'll look into it."

That afternoon: The Bridgehill Historical Society has seen better days. Its brick siding is sun-faded and cracked, and one of the pillars at the entrance is sagging. The windows are dirty, and the glassed front door has an upper pane missing.

"We don't get any funds for maintenance," says Arnold Henstrom from the open doorway. "And I'm too damn old to clean up the place. Got enough to do keepin' the files!"

He wears a frayed green sweater, is totally bald, and peers at Donner through bottle-thick glasses.

"Well, don't just stand there," says Henstrom gruffly. "Step along inside."

Donner follows the aged historian down a narrow hallway.

"I appreciate your allowing me to—"

"I'll do the talkin' ... you do the walkin'" says the old man as they enter a high-ceilinged reference room. The reading tables are deserted.

"Don't get many young folks snoopin' through here anymore," he mutters. "Guess they got better things to do.

I'm pretty much to myself these days. Got plenty a'time to jabber with you."

Henstrom waves Donner to an empty chair. "Wait here," he says, disappearing between rows of shelved reference volumes.

The old man returns bearing a large plastic-bound book of clippings. "Knew I had this dang thing back in the stacks," he declares. "Just had to recollect where to look. Tons a'books to keep track of, but I got me a memory like an elephant."

"A real asset for sure."

"You're lucky I'm a nosy old codger, Mr. Donner."

"How so?"

Henstrom chuckles. "I thrive on local mysteries. Collect data on 'em. The odd, the offbeat… that's what stirs my old bones."

"And Warwick House is offbeat?"

"You betcha. Plenty that's never been explained about what happened there."

"And what *did* happen?"

"We'll get to that, but first… " tipping back the cover of the scrapbook, "here's his nibs, Hiram Stearns Warwick himself—where it all starts."

A news clipping is taped to the page—a photo of Warwick, glowering and cold-eyed.

"Old Warwick was a shrewd gambler," says Henstrom. "He could smell money. In 1859, at 19, he found out about the big silver strike in Virginia City, and packed out for Nevada. Bought into a silver mine that paid off big. Part of the Comstock Lode. Made him wealthy overnight."

"What brought him to Connecticut?"

"Don't rightly know. He gambled on riverboats for years, rakin' in the money. Finally made up his mind to build his own private palace—an' that was Warwick House. Built it in 1902. A prime showplace. Complete with his own family cemetery."

He points out other clips. "After he died the whole shebang went to ruin. Stayed unsold till the Maitlands took it over. Nobody wanted to live there."

"So far," says Donner, "you've told me nothing that's odd—or offbeat."

"Hold your dang horses, I'm gettin' there!" He turns more pages. "Hiram had two young daughters and a small son when he moved into his new house with his wife, Prudence. In 1904 she had another daughter. Children all seemed normal 'cept for the last child. Prudence died giving birth to her."

"Wasn't death in childbirth pretty common in those days?"

"Not *this* kinda death," says Henstrom. "This baby, the one Hiram named Anna, seemed to want to *harm* its mother… fought to escape from the womb, as if her birth mother was an enemy. So, one lived, the other died."

"How did Hiram take his wife's death?"

"Hard. Real hard. Locked himself and all his children away from the world inside that big house. As the new baby daughter grew older all of the other children sickened one by one, grew weak, and died. And by the time Anna was full grown, her father, old man Warwick, also sickened and died. Passed away on Anna's thirtieth birthday.

He shows Ted a yellowed clipping:

HIRAM WARWICK DIES

Eccentric Millionaire Stricken at Warwick House

Donner studies the news article. "They call the cause of his death 'unknown'. Does anyone actually know what killed him?"

Henstrom cackles. "Nobody knows. Hah! A mystery. But he was no spring chicken, bein' nearly ninety-five."

"And what happened to the girl ... Anna?"

"Went bonkers. Totally crazy. Grief, I guess. Last of the Warwicks. Ended up in Briarhurst, the State Asylum." Henstrom flips to another page, tapping one of the news stories with a gnarled finger.

ANNA WARWICK DIES

Millionaire's Daughter Succumbs at Briarhurst

Donner frowns. "Succumbs?"

The historian nods. "Heart attack—less than six months after her papa's death. She was buried in the family cemetery behind Warwick House. Even though she was thirty, she barely looked out of her teens. And a right pretty little thing she was."

"Is there a photo of her?"

"Yessir, they ran one in the local paper ... at her burial."

He locates the clip. The woman in the photo, Anna Warwick, seems strangely familiar to Ted. "Could you make me a copy of this?"

A week goes by. Joan and Ted are just finishing dinner at the Bridgehill Cafe, seated at a corner table lit by flickering red candles. They are relaxing over wine and a cheese plate.

"So, what does 'Bathory' mean?" Joan asks.

"Well, I did some digging at the University library, hit the Internet, and talked with that old geezer Henstrom at the Bridgehill Historical Society, and found out quite a bit ... Apparently, she was an infamous countess from the seventeenth century. One of history's first documented serial killers, supposedly responsible for more than six hundred deaths."

Joan's eyes widen. "Jesus. I guess that's one way to get famous."

"They called her 'The Blood Countess'. She would lure

young girls to her castle in Hungary, then have them tortured and killed. She craved blood—drank it, even bathed in the blood of virgins—in the belief that blood would keep her from prematurely aging; that it possessed magical restorative powers…At any rate, the story goes that the family was 'cursed'; several members of their line had died young, but their bodies were withered, skeletal, literally shells of what they had been…Folktales sprang up about her and her 'activities'—it was also said that she was one of the undead."

Joan is shocked. "The 'undead'?"

"Ludicrous, I know, but so legend has it. In my classes, I discuss how planarian worms pass genetic information down from one generation to the next by way of cannibalism. Perhaps her family was demonstrating a similar phenomenon—maybe some kind of genetic blood disorder. It's not uncommon in royalty as a result of inbreeding depression. More potential for geniuses, but also more madness, more low IQs, and more diseases, like hemophilia."

"Didn't anyone try to stop her?"

"Oh, sure—and they finally did. Walled her up alive in her own castle."

"How horrible!"

"I believe she's the subject of Dave's new book. My guess is he became obsessed by the fact that the Warwicks were direct descendants of Elizabeth Bathory."

She stares at him. "How do you know that?"

"Research… I did some digging, and there's a lot about it online. Warwick family history—I traced it all the way back to the seventeenth century. And there are some pretty bizarre rumors connected with Anna's death… "

"No, no, I don't remember her," the matron declares, shaking her head. "She was just one of hundreds. They come and go."

Donner is at Briarhurst Asylum, displaying the copy of Anna's photo to Elma Viggon in her office at the asylum. Viggon's office is as stark and plain as the matron herself. She's in her nineties, hair tied back in a tight bun, granny glasses balanced on her sharp nose.

"But Anna Warwick was *a patient here?"*

"That's correct, according to the records. And we keep very accurate records. All the way back to our first year."

She takes a small metal watering can from her desk, walks over to a potted plant by the window and carefully sprinkles it. "I name all my plants," she tells Donner. "I call this one Eleanor. Seems to fit her."

"Can we talk about Anna Warwick?"

"Of course." She returns the can to her desk. "I was a floor nurse in 1925. Records show that Anna was one of my ward patients, but obviously she made no special impression on me. That was fifty years ago, Mr. Donner. How can I be expected to remember her?"

"But she died *here. Wouldn't that—"*

"Many girls have died here. That's normal."

"I understand… but can you at least tell me the precise nature of her mental illness?"

"I'm afraid that's not possible. Insanity exists in a variety of forms, Mr. Donner. In Anna's case I can say no more than that she was mentally damaged." Delicately, as if her bones were fine china, she settles herself behind the desk. "I have no other information for you, sir."

"Did she die of a heart attack?"

"The records say so."

"Surely there must be someone here who—"

"Ah… " Mrs. Viggon purses her lips. "Now that I think of it… Mira just might remember Miss Warwick."

"Mira?"

The old woman rises, moving toward the corridor. "This way."

They reach a locked door in mid-corridor. Mrs. Viggon selects a key from the belt at her waist. "Mira is our oldest guest. She was here during Anna's time. In the same ward. She just might remember."

Donner frowns. "But if she's a mental patient…"

"You'll find her mind as clear as a child's. What she may tell you can be relied upon."

She unlocks the door and they step inside.

The room is sterile white. Walls, floor, ceiling—all stark white. There's a narrow white bed, a white dresser, a small white lamp on a white end table, and a single white wooden chair. A screened toilet and wash basin complete the furnishings. A framed picture of Jesus hangs above the bed, his heart bleeding.

Mira has been lying down, and sits up in bed as they approach her.

"You have a visitor, Mira."

Mira is pale, very thin, with sparse white hair. She wears a faded blue uniform dress. She shakes her head. "Oh no, Mrs. Viggon, I never *get visitors. Never do. Never get visitors."*

"Well, you have one today. This is Mr. Donner."

Mira blinks at him.

Donner sits in the wooden chair as Mrs. Viggon prepares to leave. "When you are finished here, just press the button near the door."

She exits, the lock clicking into place behind her. Mira huddles against the wall, arms tight around her knees. She looks frightened. "What you want with me, mister?"

"I just want to talk, Mira… to ask you about someone."

"About who?" Her voice is frail, uncertain.

"A girl you knew a long time ago here at Briarhurst. See, I have her picture." He takes out Anna's photo, holds it close. Mira peers at it, then smiles, her face brightening.

"Yes, yes! That's my friend. That's Anna!"

Donner is relieved. "Then you remember her?"

"Oh, yes. We shared secrets together. We were best friends. I even know why she went away."

"Away?"

"When you die they take you away. And she wanted to do that—to die. So she made it happen."

Donner is shaken. "Anna killed *herself?"*

Mira nods. "One night—she didn't like sunlight time too much—she just laid down on the bed, closed her eyes, and didn't get up anymore. They had to carry her out. Anna made her heart stop. She knew how to do stuff like that."

"I don't see how—"

Mira cut into his words, her voice high and excited. "Told me that Anna wasn't always her name. Told me she had a real *one—a secret name—from a long, long time ago in another place."*

"Go on, Mira."

"It was a nice name… Elizabeth… Elizabeth.*" She giggles. "Isn't that a nice name?"*

Donner continues: "Some people in Bridgehill became convinced that Anna was actually a reincarnation of Elizabeth Bathory… a kind of 'modern-day vampire'. After she died, they dug up her coffin and drove a stake through her heart."

"You've *got* to be kidding."

Ted smiles thinly. "A little barbaric, I'll admit—but superstition can cause people to do some incredible things."

"Do you believe Dave knows about… all this?" Joan asks him.

"I think that's why he bought Warwick House."

"But what made him turn so secretive?"

"Only Dave has the answer to that." Ted pushes his plate

aside, finishing his wine. "I'm going out to Warwick House tonight, and I hope to learn more."

"You're going to see Dave?"

He shakes his head. "No, this time ... not Dave."

Later that night, as thick velvet darkness cloaks Warwick House, Ted parks his car well short of the mansion and makes his way quietly to the rear. He reaches the family cemetery, a weathered, moon-shadowed area of white marble tombstones. A night wind moans through the high grass, and around Donner the trees twist and lash their branches.

He carries a flashlight. Ted running its beam across several of the tombstones, over the names:

PRUDENCE ELVIRA WARWICK
1870-1904
Beloved Wife

HIRAM STEARNS WARWICK
1840-1934
Husband

EDWARD REDDING WARWICK
1898-1917

MELANIE THAXTON WARWICK
1900-1918

CHARITY LOUISE WARWICK
1901-1919

Finally, the beam illuminates:

ANNA MARIE WARWICK
1904-1934

Donner places the light on a ledge, removes a shovel from his car, and begins digging up Anna's coffin. Grunting with effort, he succeeds in unearthing it after a few long, sweaty hours. He pauses to regain his breath, standing above the coffin.

So far, so good…

He tugs at the lid. It slides off with a hollow grinding sound. He picks up the flashlight, shines it into the coffin.

The interior is empty: Anna's body is gone. *No bones. Nothing.*

Ted directs the beam to one corner of the coffin—to illuminate a rotted wooden stake.

He reaches for it, turns it slowly under the lamp. It is crusted with black.

Anna Warwick's blood… Or someone else's?

Donner pulls out his cell phone and calls Joan's apartment.

Ring…

Ring…

Ring…

A few moments past midnight at The Forum, Bridgehill's local movie theater: The cashier, Karen Sutton, a pretty girl just out of her teens, is locking up for the night. She holds the street door open for a balding old man, Abe Steiner. "Glad you enjoyed the movie, Mr. Steiner."

"Sure did." He gives her a toothless smile. "I like them Westerns. Never get tired of them Westerns. Lotsa ridin' an' shootin' and bar fightin'… yes ma'am, never get tired of them Westerns."

He hobbles off into the darkness.

Karen switches out the light in the cashier's cage, does the same with the popcorn machine. One dim bulb is left burning over the outside door. She crosses the lobby, parting the curtains to enter the auditorium.

Inside a woman is seated alone in the front row of the otherwise empty auditorium, her back to Karen. She is dressed in black, unmoving, facing the blank movie screen.

Karen walks to her down the aisle. "Sorry, but the show's over. You'll have to leave now. We're locking up."

No response. No movement.

Karen is annoyed. "Did you *hear* me? The show's over."

Now she is directly behind the woman, who slowly pivots around: Her face glows with a dreadful blood lust, her lips drawn back over shark-sharp teeth as her dark eyes fix on the young cashier.

Terrified, Karen wheels around, running up the aisle into the lobby. Abruptly, she is seized in strong arms; crushed in a terrible embrace, Karen finds her voice at last…

Until her screams are cut short, dying in the ruins of her throat.

Cruising past The Forum in his patrol car, Deputy Stoddard happens to hear Karen. He stops the car, jumps out, and runs into the lobby, gun in hand.

Inside, he stops short: The lobby is empty. Uncertain, the lawman moves toward the heavy green curtain leading to the auditorium. Thick silence. The lobby is dim and menacing, illumined only by the single light bulb above the door.

Suddenly, the curtain whips back, and Deputy Blanchard glares out at his fellow officer, hands bloody, his mouth twisted. The front of his uniform is caked with red from his mangled neck.

"Blanchard! We have an APB out for you. Found your

squad car out on Shannon Road, engine still running. I don't get it. What happened to—"

Stoddard hesitates; his voice trails off as he sees, behind Blanchard, Anna Warwick—with an arm around Karen's sagging, bloodied figure.

At that moment, Blanchard lunges forward, eyes ablaze, reaching for the other deputy. Stoddard fires at him, and the bullet buries itself in the tall man's chest. Blanchard keeps coming. Stoddard fires four more rounds, but the shots have no effect on the deputy…

Clawed hands close on Stoddard's windpipe.

At a press conference the following morning, an excited cluster of news reporters crowd Jim Baxter's office. The sheriff looks flustered, under obvious pressure to answer their questions.

"Is it true that there was a lot of blood found in the lobby of the Forum?"

Baxter shakes his head. "I have no information on that. At the moment we don't know what happened inside that theater."

"Do you believe that Karen Sutton is still alive?"

"I have no way of knowing. She's missing. Period."

"And what about, your two deputies, Stoddard and Blanchard?"

"No comment."

"Meaning you have no clue to their whereabouts, is that it, Sheriff Baxter?"

"I *said* no comment."

"And what about the school teacher, Peggy Ames?" asks a female reporter. "She able to talk yet?"

"Unfortunately, no. Ms. Ames is now with her parents."

Professor Donner stands in the doorway as Baxter waves off the reporters. "Sorry, people, but that's all I have to say." To Donner: "Come on in."

Ted enters as Baxter crosses to his desk to light a fresh cigar. He looks weary. "They're like a wolf pack, the way they hang on a man. They expect me to have all the answers … and I don't."

"I wouldn't trade jobs with you."

Baxter grunts, then: "So, what's on your mind, Professor? Sounded urgent on the phone."

Donner takes a chair facing the desk. "What I have to say may seem … illogical. But bear with me, it's important."

"Try me. I'm paid to listen."

"Let's begin with the fact that you're looking for this mystery woman. The suspect."

"Do you have a line on her?"

"Just listen." Ted draws in a breath. "I've been doing a lot of research on the Warwicks … into Anna Warwick in particular."

"I know the name," nods Baxter. "She had a heart attack at Briarhurst not long after old Warwick bit the bullet. Died in the State Asylum."

"Right. I believe she killed her father and faked her own death."

Baxter looks skeptical. "How do you 'fake' a heart attack?"

"It's been done." Ted nods, understanding the sheriff's concern. "For example, a yogi can arrest the heart, lower blood pressure, simulate death. I think that's what Anna did."

"Go on, Mr. Donner. I'm enjoying your little discourse. Gets better all the time," Baxter proclaims.

"I think Anna Warwick has returned … And I think she is behind these disappearances." His tone is determined. "I think she's done something to Dave Maitland … It's like he's totally under her power."

"She use drugs on him?"

"Don't know … Maybe. She definitely seems to have some kind of 'hypnotic' control over Maitland, though."

"Let me get this straight," says Baxter. "She was thirty when she died, and that was sixty or so years ago. That makes her over ninety. She's a pretty active old gal."

Ted holds the Sheriff's gaze. "Well, maybe she has a distant relative that wants revenge, or to get the house… Maybe this relative is obsessed with Anna Warwick or something—hell, I don't know! *Whoever* it is, I think they attacked Deputy Blanchard—and after that Karen Sutton, at the theater. Obviously got to Stoddard, too. All of them are missing. I think all victims of the same person."

Baxter grins. "So that's your theory?"

"Well… I have no proof. But, based on some research I'm working on, I think whoever this person is *believes* they're Anna Warwick… And possibly thinks they are a vampire."

"*Vampire?* That's crazy, Donner."

Ted smiles. "Agreed. But madness and disease run in the Warwick family. And there *are* mental illnesses where people *believe* they need blood… " He sees the distaste on the Sheriff's face, but continues. "For example, porphyria, is an iron disorder of the blood which causes folks to avoid sunlight; makes their skin become photosensitive, their eyes and gums bleed… Hell, even rabies can cause hyper-sexuality, hydrophobia, bloody frothing at the mouth—not to mention aggression, biting, scratching, and so on… There was also a famous case in California about a guy with a form of schizophrenia. Name was Richard Chase. They called him 'The Vampire of Sacramento'. He was intensely violent—ate a baby, thought he needed blood to keep his head from changing shape due to signals sent from the past by Nazis… "

Baxter looks at Donner, then chuckles. "Professor, I'd say you've got one heck of an imagination. What the hell do you care, anyway?"

Ted is taken aback. "Well, Dave was my best friend . . . And, anyhow, it's personal."

"I see. I think it's Joan—you fancy her, I think." Baxter looks askance at Donner, who doesn't reply. "So what do you want from me?" the Sheriff asks finally.

Donner stands. "I want to see Ms. Ames."

"What for? She's out of it. Doesn't respond to questions. What good's she gonna do you?"

"I'd still like to see her."

"Okay," sighs Baxter, "guess it can't hurt."

"Hello?" The old woman's voice is frail over the line.

"Yes, Mrs. Ames? My name is Professor Ted Donner. I am a friend of a friend and I would like to visit Peggy."

The line is silent.

Donner: "I know this is a shock, but I think I can get through to Ms. Ames, and I need her help to identify a person I think was involved with the incident with poor Mr. Clark."

The old woman clears her throat. "I'm sorry Professor Donner. I can't help you."

"I understand the sensitive nature of what happened with Ms. Ames, but this is a matter of life and death."

He can hear the woman crying on the other end of the line. He speaks again softening his tone: "Please, Mrs. Ames . . . "

"I would like to help you, Professor Donner . . . but I can't . . . " Mrs. Ames is sobbing openly now. "Peggy just died an hour ago . . . "

Joan tosses and turns in a frustrated effort to sleep. It's impossible. Propping herself on one elbow, she switches on the bed lamp at the night table, checks the alarm clock: 1am.

This can't go on. I won't let it go on.

She gets up in her nightgown, moves into the front room,

stares at a framed photo on the mantle—a picture taken of Joan and Dave on their honeymoon. Holding hands, they smile happily out at the photographer. A shared moment of joy.

Joan turns away, returns to the bedroom, and begins dressing.

She has a destination in mind.

Ted Donner abruptly pulls to the curb in front of Joan's building and walks quickly into the lobby. He rings the buzzer to her apartment. *No answer.*

A night watchman emerges from a back room.

Ted turns to him. "Is Joan Maitland in? She's not answering her phone. I haven't been able to reach her for days."

"Heck if I know. If she's not answering . . . "

"I need to find her. Did you see her leave?"

"Nope."

"Can you take me up to her door?"

"Sorry. Only allowed to take authorities up if the tenant ain't answering . . . "

Donner's face is tight; the muscle along his lower jaw is rigid. He pulls out his cell phone and dials the sheriff.

Baxter answers: "Yeah?"

"It's me, Sheriff."

"Christ, Donner! It's almost three in the morning. Are you crazy?"

"I'm calling about Joan."

"What about her?"

"She's not in her apartment. I wondered if you might know where she is."

"She called me earlier tonight, all upset over Dave. Asked if I thought he was involved in these murders."

"What did you tell her?"

"That there was no evidence to support that idea. She said she couldn't take the way things are going between them, so I told her to go see him and straighten this mess out facetoface."

Donner is stunned. "You told her to go there—to Warwick House?"

"Sure I did. He's her husband isn't he? Don't see what's wrong with—"

Donner is on his way out of the lobby, running for his car.

Joan arrives at Warwick House, stopping her car a few yards from the entrance. She gets out, stands for a moment in the cricketing darkness. She gazes up at the looming mansion: A single light glows from the window of the downstairs library.

Where Dave always works on his damn book…

She crosses the brush-tangled lawn, mounts the steps, and moves along the creaking porch until she reaches the library window. Peering inside, she sees Dave, in profile, at his desk. He is facing the typewriter, a drink in his hand. His clothes are ragged and stained. His head is tipped back, eyes closed. There's an empty bottle of whiskey on the table.

Is he dozing or is he drunk?

Joan tries the sliding library door. *Locked.* She taps on the glass. Startled, Dave swings around in his chair, sees Joan. Unsteadily, he walks to the door to slide it open.

His voice is harsh: "What are you doing here? I told you never—"

Joan overrides his words. "I *had* to see you!"

She attempts to embrace him, but he flinches back. "Why have you come?"

"To talk," she says. "We have to talk."

"There's nothing to talk about." He glares at her. "You were a fool to come here alone at night."

He stumbles toward his desk, removes a fresh bottle of

whiskey from a top drawer, and pours himself another drink. “This is all wrong, you being here.”

“You make it sound as if I’m in some kind of danger.”

“You *are!*” He gestures toward the door. “Go back to your car and leave. Now.”

Her eyes flash defiance. “Not until I have some answers as to why all this is happening to us!”

He grabs her arm, propels her toward the door. “I said *leave!*”

She twists away from him, face flushed with anger. “Why haven’t you tried to see me?”

“I don’t see anyone anymore. It’s all over between us. Can’t you understand that?”

“I understand it, but I won’t *accept* it.” She hesitates, her voice softening. “I think you still love me.”

“And what if I do? That doesn’t change anything.” He looks over her shoulder at the shadowed hallway. “There’s no time to argue. You *must* drive away from here. Every second you stay in this house you’re risking—”

“Just what am I risking, Dave?”

“Don’t question me. I can’t—” He grips both her arms in desperation. “Joanfor God’s sake*will* you go?”

“Not without a reason.”

“You want a reason … all right, I’ll give you one. If you stay here and they find you, you’ll *die*. Is that reason enough?”

“Who are *they?*”

He looks pale, defeated. “I’m responsible for all of this … the two deputies … the girl … even for the death of old man Clark at the school.”

She steps back, in shock, staring at him. “Then Ted was right … you *are* involved!”

“What did he tell you?”

“That … somehow … Anna Warwick is alive … that she’s

behind these attacks... and that you're helping her."

He looks anguished. "I didn't *want* to. Swear to God I didn't. But she promised to spare me—and you—if I'd... " His voice reflects deep pain. "During my investigation of her life for my book, I became enamored of her story... I thought that she might be misunderstood. Was it a superstitious myth? Mental illness? A disease? What was behind it? Doesn't matter now. Anyway, I brought her back to life by accident. I learned about the stake, thought it was all bullshit, but when I found it there, in her grave and buried in her chest, I pulled it free... "

He slumps into the desk chair, hands to his face.

Joan is confused. "Then you—"

"I discovered that it wasn't a legend... not a superstition... not some disorder. Anna came to me that night... young... beautiful... all-consuming... and each night since... "

His words, like knives, cut into Joan.

"What are you saying?"

"Anna Warwick, like her ancestor Elizabeth Bathory, is a *true* vampire—one of the undead. She needs the blood of her victims to live... Vampires—*they're real, Joan!*" He stares up at his wife with pain-filled eyes. "When I pulled out that stake... I freed her!"

A soft rustle of sound from the hallway. A bare whisper—but enough to panic Dave Maitland. He springs up from the desk to push Joan toward the sliding door.

Deputy Blanchard confronts them from the hall, his face shining with a fearsome inner fire. Anna Warwick glides past him into the room, her eyes smoldering, feral, deadly.

"No, no!" cries Dave, stepping in front of Joan. "Not this one... not her!"

Anna's gaze is fastened, in red hunger, on Joan.

Two others materialize in the hallway next to Blanchard: Karen Sutton and Wayne Stoddard. They are both in blood heat, savoring the imminent kill.

Joan huddles at Dave's shoulder, weak with terror. "Don't … don't let them touch me!"

Dave blinks, his muscles taut, struggling to resist the spellbinding power of Anna Warwick. He steps away from Joan, speaking slowly, spacing his words in a flat, emotionless voice: "She won't … hurt you, Joan … you'll only feel … pleasure … not pain. Open yourself to her."

Shocked by Dave's words, Joan pivots to the table, her fingers closing around a heavy brass bookend. She raises it, but, snake-quick, Anna knocks the weapon from Joan's hand, then leans toward her fear-numbed victim.

"Time to feed."

Sweating, trembling, Dave manages to break the spell, placing himself between Joan and her attacker. "Leave … her … alone!"

With a guttural snarl, Anna smashes her fist into Dave's chest, pulling his beating heart from his ribcage. He gives a muted cry as she thrusts it into his bloody startled face, still pulsing in her twisted fingers, before tossing it to Karen, Blanchard, and Stoddard. She cackles with glee as he falls to the rug.

Running for her life, Joan bolts across the room to an open door leading down to the wine cellar. She darts inside, jerks the door closed and snap-locks it, then staggers, half-falling, down the bricked stairs.

From the library side, the creatures furiously batter at the thinlypaneled door. It shudders under their attack.

Trapped in the cellar, Joan's breath is ragged; she is close to an emotional breaking point. Frantically, her heart pounding, she scans the area for a way out.

A window!

She runs between rows of dusty wine bottles, toward the dim circle of light from a glassed cellar window.

The window is too small for her to crawl through. She raises her head to the battering sounds from above.

That door won't hold for much longer!

In the dimness of the room, she bumps into a massive, bulky object. Joan gasps.

It's an open coffin, filled with worm-riddled grave dirt, one of four spaced over the damp cellar floor. Foul homes for the undead. A fat gray rat emerges from one of them, scampering into darkness.

Backing away from the coffins, she discovers an axe handle, the cutting edge missing, half-buried in a mound of grave dirt. Upstairs, with a splintering crash, the door gives way, as the night creatures swarm the landing. They are on her.

Anna's clawed hand closes on Joan's neck. She twists around, raises the axe handle and sends the woman reeling back from a tremendous blow. Swinging wildly at the others, she fights through the creatures in a melée of horror. Gasping for breath, she scrambles up the steps leading from the wine cellar to the house.

Reaching her car, she jumps in, fumbling under the floor mat for a spare ignition key. The beasts emerge from the house, rushing toward her, shrieking.

She guns the car forward, tires spitting gravel, Joan whip-spins the machine, aiming at the advancing night creatures, led by Anna. The front fender slams into Deputy Stoddard, spinning him sideways, but the others manage to leap aside as Joan bullets onto the grooved woods road.

In her panic, crouched over the wheel, she is driving much too fast. A deep rut sends her car sliding wildly. The speeding vehicle slews off the road surface into a weed-choked ditch, front wheels buried in heavy, clogging brush. Joan is dazed but unhurt.

Got to keep moving—they'll be here soon!

Unable to back out, she cuts the engine, pushes open the door and exits the car, sobbing in frustration. She begins running in a half-stumble along the woods road, exhausted upon reaching asphalt.

Headlights!

Illuminated in the oncoming flare of the beams, Joan waves desperately. The car pulls to a stop beside her. The words BRIDGEHILL POLICE are on the door.

A miracle, that's all it is—a miracle!

At the car window, her gratitude flows out in a rush of quick-spoken, breathless words: "Thank God you're here! … I've been … at the house … they tried to kill me … turn me into one of them … I escaped but … my car is in the ditch … "

Her voice falters. She stares at the officer in the dim interior of the patrol car. He sits rigidly at the wheel, saying nothing. The car's engine ticks quietly in the darkness.

Joan climbs into the rear seat. "Please *go* … we need to get away from here."

The car starts moving—turning onto the dirt road.

"No! Wrong way! You're heading right for them! Get help. They're very strong. You won't be able to—"

Her voice fails as the driver turns around to smile at her. His fangs are dagger-sharp.

"Let's go for a ride," says Deputy Fred Blanchard.

Ted Donner brakes to a sudden stop next to Joan's ditched automobile.

Ted looks inside the vehicle, making sure that Joan is not trapped there. Finding it empty, he returns to his car and continues down the dirt road, frowning and obviously disturbed.

Where the hell is she?

Donner pulls up Warwick Hill, wheeling into the gravel area fronting the house. He slides to a stop and kills the engine. Exiting the car, silence envelops him. The lightening dawn sky is gray, cloudy.

At the entrance, he rattles the knob, then bangs the devil's-head knocker against the oak door, shouting: "Joan! Dave—open up. It's me, Ted. Open the damn door!

"No answer." Donner mutters under his breath, moving along the porch to a leaded front window. He wraps a kerchief around his fist and smashes out the glass. He steps inside. "Joan! Dave! Are you here?"

He walks rapidly through the vast mansion, checking each room. No sign of Joan or Dave. He pauses in front of the hideous painting in the grand hallway, studying the gruesome image of sexual frenzy.

Is it a warning?

Back on the lower floor, he enters the library—and is shocked to find Dave's mutilated body sprawled on the rug. His friend's dead eyes stare out blankly. Ted kneels to examine the corpse.

Someone sure did a job on him. Jesus…

He notices the splintered cellar door. Descends the stairs—drawn by a soft whimpering. The sound is repeated.

Then he finds…

"Joan!"

She's bound securely with rope, an old rag covering her mouth. Her top is bloodied and her face is smudged with dirt. Her eyes bug out wildly as Donner cuts the rope away with a pocketknife. Once freed, she throws her arms around his neck, hugging him close.

"Ted, thank God… I never thought that anyone would find me! I fought them and escaped, but they got me on the road … After they tied me up, I must have passed out … "

She breaks into tears, her body quivering in his arms.

"Who are 'they'?" he asks.

She gestures toward the coffins in a far corner of the cellar. "Those *things*."

Ted tips back the lid on the largest coffin, and stares down at Anna Warwick: she is lying in the casket, her mouth bloody, her cloudy eyes open. He checks the other boxes and finds them occupied by Blanchard, Stoddard, and the teenager, Karen.

"She … " Joan pauses, touching the side of her neck. "She … *ate* Dave's heart … It was horrible! Anyway, Dave said that he released her when he pulled a stake from her chest … It brought her to life again," Joan said.

"And the others?"

"The two deputies, Stoddard and Blanchard … the girl, Karen … Dave said that she had drained their blood … That she made them all like her."

"What about Dave? Was he one of them, too?"

"No, she used him as a kind of … *slave* … kept him under her spell … She killed him when he tried to help me. I guess we need to call Sheriff Baxter … have him come out here."

Donner shakes his head. "No—before we leave here we must deal with this ourselves."

"And do what?"

He looks down at Anna's coffin, remembering the grisly painting in the hallway, finally grasping its meaning. "What has to be done … "

Ted and Joan are seated in his car. He starts the engine and the vehicle rolls down the gravel drive.

"Is it really over, Ted? Can they … somehow … come back?"

Ted pats her on the leg, she takes his hand in hers, as they motor down the road, back to sanity. A stray thought causes him to smile. *I guess the best man finally won after all.* He glances at her as she reclines in the passenger seat, eyes closed, rubbing her temple.

"My research indicated that 'vampires' need corporal bodies to function. I learned that if you staked their bodies to the earth, removed their hearts, or you cut off their head, that's the end of them . . . Of course, if you slice off *anything's* head, that's the end of it! Anna Warwick and the others . . . they won't be coming back. By the way, how's that cut on your neck?"

She reaches up, feeling the injury on her throat. "It stopped bleeding, but still feels kind of warm, tingly . . . "

Ted swallows, his smile fading. "We'll have it checked as soon as we get to town." He looks ahead into the overcast morning sky as he wheels the car onto the highway.

They never reached the city.

This one is Nolan-out-of-Virgil-out-of-Homer. Virgil was the popular name given to the famed Roman poet Publius Vergilios Maro. His enduring classic, the epic Aeneid, *inspired me to write "Dread Voyage". But I must also salute Homer whose* Iliad *and* Odyssey(*both of which, in turn, had inspired Virgil*) *were also solidly in mind as I wrote.*

The confrontation with Circe, the dark enchantress who held the power to turn men into animals, is more Homer than Virgil. She was a goddess in Greek mythology, a daughter of the Sun, living on the isle of Aeaea. A very nasty lady indeed.

—WFN

DREAD VOYAGE

And so it came to pass that
Diocreasas, son of Aeneas, (he that was born
Of man and goddess) set out from
Fair Italian shore on a tall ship to cross
The storm-bent blue-green sea.

His goal be vengeance. Girdled for battle,
In gilded shield and armored gold, bronze sword belted,
He would have harsh traffic with fierce-eyed Circe,
Siren queen and sorceress, she whose
Arcane magic turned brave men to swine, to ape,
To snuffling boar, she who transformed, most
Horribly, good men of Trojan birth, she
Who held their souls in darkest thrall.

Diocreasas, son of Aeneas, in righteous anger,
Swearing revenge, sought wise counsel with Venus,
Beloved of Olympus, daughter of Jupiter, wife
To Vulcan, mother to Cupid, she who birthed
His life-gone father, now a Shade in the lands
Of night, lost to son and loving goddess.

"Most noble Venus, I implore thee. Aid me in
My quest, to strike down she whose seductive siren
Voice drew forth the faithful men of Troy to
Bestial form. Assist me, by your vaunted powers,
To rid the world of this foul creature.
Lend strength to my resolve, that such a horror
Shall taste the meat of vengeance, as she doth
Savor the sour wine of death upon my good blade.
For this, I pledge great gifts upon your altar."

And Venus did in turn reply: "What you ask of me,
Brave Diocreasas, I would gladly grant
Were my powers of equal weight against witching
Circe. Alas, her powers pass mine, and I am
Helpless in your worthy cause. You must, then, voyage
To her isle, full-sail in your tall ship, and
By your strength of mind and heart, destroy
This vile enchantress. But beware! In warning
I adjure you, look not into her eyes,
For there doth dwell her dark-held magic.
Meet not her evil gaze, lest you find yourself
A snorting swine." And thus
Upon this somber warning, Venus
Quick departed in a cloud that rode
The sky-blue heavens to Olympus.

So, in full sail, Diocreasas, with his crew of nine,
Did set out, by day and night, to cross the
Vasty sea, his fateful passage sore-marked by
Juno, ever enemy to all Trojans. She swift-sought
Sea god Neptune, ruler of the blue-green waves,
Inciting him to act.
"Loose the gusting winds against this bold

Son of Troy," she soft implored. "Pile high
The killing waves, till his tall ship
Shall split and founder."
And Neptune, no friend to Diocreasas, called down
The lightning and fierce gales in cruel assault.

The tall ship, clutched by storm, shed its
Tattered sail, timbered hull deep-buried
In spume-tossed brine. Yet Diocreasas,
Stalwart at the helm, held fast his course,
Until, weary of the game, old Neptune
Retired to sleep, putting the storm to rest
Upon the bosom of his blue-green waters.

Aurora, goddess of the dawn, sent her
Pale radiance as guide to Diocreasas
In his quest for Circe's isle.
A day, a night, another day, and goal
Achieved, Diocreasas beached his ship to
Step ashore and enter sere woods,
Deep-tangled and bewitched. His crew
He left behind, fearful of their safety
In this dark endeavor.

Warned by Juno of the Trojan's coming,
Circe quick departed her webbed cave. How dare
This foolish son of Troy bring threat to *her!*
Confident of triumph, secure of great magic, she
Strode forth to render him to swine. Behind,
Draped in tapered shadow, beast-men
Howled and grumbled.

Diocreasas, cautioned by the words of Venus,
Averted his gaze once met with Circe
Within the brooding wood. Green fire sparking
Her eyes, Circe taunted with mocking voice:
"Why stand with lowered head, my Trojan. I am
But frail woman. Surely, in your manly
Strength, you need have no fear of me."

He made swift reply: "You deceive me not. Indeed,
Your eyes hold dread power. You would make
Of me a beast. Lo! I shall not succumb
To such foul witchery."
"Then be torn limb from limb!" she cried, raising
A hand to summon forth those who had been men
Now turned sharp-toothed savage.

In desperate mode, Diocreasas leapt forward
To plunge his ready sword into
Circe's pale throat, the blade hard-driven to
Penetrate her chambered brain and split
Her sundered skull across.
In crimson tide, she fell to rooted earth. And at
Her fall, the creatures paused full on
In rough assault, reverting back to form,
Regaining the humanity stolen from them.

Vengeance had been wrought.
The men of Troy were free.
There is no more to tell.

I have written several stories featuring the iconic detective Sherlock Holmes, but never one like this. Holmes himself is not actually present here, but his archenemy, James Moriarty, certainly is. I doubt that he's the Moriarty that Conan Doyle would recognize, though.

Here, then, a story that's "outside the box," a deft (I would hope) mix of possible truth in place of iconic legend.

—WFN

FLIGHT TO LEGEND

All this, what I'm about to tell you, beginning with the "urgent" cablegram right through the crazed ending, happened a long time ago. In 1935, to be exact.

Why am I writing about it now? Because folks keep pestering me to put down the story of how I met Moriarty. Yes, *the* Moriarty, the fellow Conan Doyle dubbed "London's master of crime" and stuck into his Sherlock Holmes nonsense. Well, perhaps not nonsense to some people, but nonsense to me. I have a strong dislike for fiction, and for detective stories in particular. Lot of claptrap and baloney. Holmes was a bore. I tried to read *The Hound of the Baskervilles,* which is supposed to be one of Doyle's best novels, got halfway into it, and threw the damn book across the room.

But I'm off the point. It's Moriarty I want to write about, the real Moriarty, but first, there are some things you need to know about me, about how I got involved in this whole insane business…

It began in Kenya, East Africa—in Nairobi, where I worked as a bush pilot, ferrying rich playboys on scenic flights over the Great Rift Valley, on to Mount Kilimanjaro and the Serengeti Plain. Didn't make much money. Barely enough for petrol and bangers, but I enjoyed flying, so this was a way to get paid for doing what I loved to do. You're free up there in the sky, away from all the petty ills of civilization. It's a *pure* feeling, being above Earth. Restores the spirit. Good for the soul.

I never worked for a safari. The ivory trade was flourishing back then and cold-hearted bastards came to Africa from all parts of the world to shoot elephants. Same as how they wiped out the buffalo back in the Old West. The way these rich playboys killed elephants, cutting off their tusks and leaving the bodies to rot in the sun… well, it made me sick. Still does, when I think about it. But, sad to say, there was nothing I could do to change things.

Met Hemingway a couple of times. Insisted I called him Papa. Egocentric, full of himself. Phony macho. Liked to boast about all the animals he'd killed. Called himself a sportsman, but slaughtering innocent animals is no sport. Without his wife's money, he could never have afforded his damn safaris. Pauline was rich, so Hemingway, who always sucked up to Big Money, took advantage of that. His *Green Hills of Africa* is horse manure. I know the *true* Africa.

Dammit! I'm off the point again!

A cablegram from London, signed "Bell," was the reason I left Nairobi.

URGENT YOU FLY HERE. CRISIS.
NEED YOU TO STOP MAJOR CRIME.
DESPERATE. COME AT ONCE.

I'd met Bell shortly before I resigned as police inspector with Scotland Yard and left London for East Africa. Like Hemingway, Bell was full of himself. I encountered him in the line of duty. He had received several threats to his life (deranged letters) and I was sent to investigate. Nothing came of the case since I was unable to trace the source. And that seemed to be the end of it—until I received his cablegram, which I answered the same day:

AM NO LONGER WITH YARD.
SUGGEST YOU CONTACT THEM.

Bell persisted with a second cable:

POLICE REFUSE TO ACT. ENTIRE
CITY OF LONDON IN DANGER.
SITUATION DIRE. DEPEND ON YOU.

I wrestled with my conscience. England was over six thousand miles away. I didn't want to make the flight, but I felt I had no moral choice. If the people of London really needed me…

I sent a three-word cable to Bell.

ON MY WAY.

I was flying a closed-cabin custom Vega Gull, which I'd fitted with extra fuel tanks. Powered by a De Havilland Gipsy engine. Totally dependable. Never any problems with one, and I didn't expect any on the flight to London.

I took off at dawn and headed due north. I had to cross Anglo-Egyptian Sudan, then fly over Egypt, across the Libyan desert to Benghazi, on to the Gulf of Sidra, to Tripoli, Tunisia, over the Mediterranean to France, and, finally, across the Channel to England. A long trip, but I'd flown it before.

The flight was smooth and trouble free and I found myself enjoying it. A storm over France created some turbulence, but the Vega was able to weather it easily.

Fog had laid a damp shroud over Croydon Airport in South London but I was able to land without incident.

A taxi took me to Edward Bell's flat just off Hampton Court. He opened the door, looking pale and distraught, a tall man in his mid-fifties with haunted eyes.

"Thank God you're here," he declared, waving me inside. "I had no one else to turn to. The police didn't believe my story."

"What *is* your story?"

"It's quite complex," said Bell, gesturing toward an antique chair. "Please, sit down. Will you have some sherry? I need a drink."

We had sherry.

"Now that you are here, I feel there is hope for London," he told me with a wan smile. "I'm sure you will be able to stop him."

"Who?"

"Professor James Moriarty."

"But that name is fictional," I said. "From Sherlock Holmes. Moriarty was—

"—the Napoleon of crime," Bell finished. "That's what Holmes called him. Let me assure you, Moriarty is not fictional. He is quite real. Lives right here in London. He is the one who sent me those death threats. Admitted it, bold as brass. Oh, he is real enough, damn his black heart!"

"Look, old fellow, I really don't—"

Bell had been pacing the room like a caged animal. Now he paused near the fireplace, pivoting to face me. "Hear me out, man! We haven't much time and there is much you need to know."

I sighed. "All right. I'm listening."

"This began in 1870, when Conan Doyle met Moriarty, who was then in his early twenties. They were both attending Stonyhurst College in Lancashire. Doyle had no knowledge at the time that his classmate would turn into the very incarnation of evil."

"Wasn't Doyle a Londoner? He placed Holmes *here,* in Baker Street."

"No, no." Bell shook his head. "Doyle was a Scot. Born in Edinburgh in 1859. He didn't become a resident of London until 1891, five years after he created Holmes. 'Sherlock' came from the Irish village of Sherlockstown, and 'Holmes' from author and poet Oliver Wendell Holmes."

"I didn't know that."

"You *do* know, of course, that without my family, Holmes would not exist."

"What do you mean?"

His voice rose on a note of pride. "My late father, Joseph Bell, was senior surgeon at Edinburgh University's Medical School when Doyle was a student there in the late 1870s. My father used the power of deduction, which greatly impressed Doyle. Thus, my father became Sherlock Holmes."

"How did he feel about being the model for the world's most famous detective?"

"We never spoke of it. I'm not sure he knew. Doubt that my father ever read a Holmes story; he was no fan of crime fiction."

"Nor am I." I dug out my pipe. "May I smoke?"

"Absolutely not. I detest the stink of tobacco."

"What about Doyle's character of Dr. Watson?" I asked. "Another college source?"

"Patrick Heron Watson was a medical rival of my father's at the university. Conan Doyle knew him there."

"Doyle originally practiced as a doctor, right?"

"Correct. He gave up medicine when his writing became successful."

"And all this leads to Moriarty?"

"Precisely. Conan Doyle's portrait of this fiend is horribly accurate."

"You say he admitted making threats on your life?"

"Yes, yes!" Bell nodded his head in rapid, bird-like motion. "He obviously hates what Doyle wrote about him and blames my family. He's quite mad, of course."

"And he's involved in this … crisis?"

Bell stood over me, his eyes blazing. His tone had risen to a pitch of near-hysteria. "That's it! Moriarty plans to poison London's water supply, using a deadly substance which is odorless and tasteless."

"When does he intend to implement his plan?"

"Tonight! At midnight! If he is not stopped before midnight, the people of London are doomed! I'm not strong enough to deal with him, but *you* are."

"Do you know where I can find him?"

"Oh, yes. He makes no secret of his whereabouts. He has a flat near Earl's Court Road." Bell scribbled the address and thrust the paper at me. "You must act *now!*" He opened a desk drawer and handed me a revolver. "Here. You had best be armed. Moriarty is a most dangerous man."

I put the weapon in my coat pocket and, with a fast-beating heart, took a taxi to Earl's Court Road.

I was about to clash with one of the world's master criminals.

When I rang the bell at Moriarty's flat, a rasping voice instantly responded: "Go away!"

Undaunted, I moved to a front window. It was unlocked. I raised the window and climbed through.

The interior was dim, with a sharp odor of decay permeating the flat. I moved cautiously down a narrow hallway, my fingers closed around the gun in my coat pocket.

The bedroom was to the left, and Moriarty's angry voice revealed his presence there: "Damn you! I told you to go away!"

I entered the room, weapon in hand.

A wizened old man glared at me from the bed. His body was emaciated, all bone and raw gristle. His skull-thin face displayed the ravages of illness and age and a patchy white beard covered his lower jaw like a fungus. He continued to glare. "Why are you pointing that thing at me?"

It was obvious that the old fellow posed no danger. I returned the revolver to my coat pocket. "Are you James Moriarty?"

"That I am. What the devil do you want, breaking in on me like this?"

I stared at him. "I want the poison."

His sunken eyes glittered. "*What* poison?"

"Don't play innocent with me. The game's up, Moriarty. Where's the stuff you intend to use against London?"

The old man began to cackle; his skeletal body shook with mirth. "So you believed him? That fool Bell?"

"He told me that you intend to poison London's water supply. Where is the poison?"

More cackling from the old man. "There is no poison. Never was."

"I don't understand."

"Edward Bell is a pompous ass. Always prattling on about how his father was the real Sherlock Holmes and how great his family is. I decided to wind him up … vex him jolly good. Bogus death threats. They got him all upset and nervous. Then I came up with this water-supply thing. Sent him cryptic messages, telling him what I planned to do to London. He fell for it all the way, damn fool that he is."

"Then you don't really plan to—"

"—poison London's water supply? Of course not. For one thing, I wouldn't know where to begin. Crikey, I can't even get out of bed!"

"You *are* the legendary James Moriarty?"

"Said so, didn't I? Yes, I knew Conan Doyle at school, and he took my name for his arch villain. But I'm no master criminal. Just a simple man—been a clerk all of my life. Handled freight statistics for a shipping company on the Thames, till my health failed." He glared at me again. "Well … now that you know the truth, why are you standing there? Get the hell out of my flat and let an old man die in peace."

I did as he ordered: I got the hell out of his flat.

The next day I flew back to Nairobi.

I wrote this story as an exercise in personal therapy, with no market in mind. As with my protagonist, I was "isolated" in Bend, Oregon, with just one friend in town (who was on the road most of the time). I had no family, with both of my parents deceased. My friends had died exactly as described in the story. (I even used their real names.) I was alone, cut off from society. The constant snow added to my depressed state.

Then, suddenly one afternoon, I realized that I had no valid reason for self-pity, that actually, I was getting along just fine. The depression lifted. I was back to normal, and my creative life resumed. I had made an important change, and "Getting Along Just Fine" celebrates that change. A nod of gratitude to my dear pal and fellow writer, Jason V Brock, for his vital "snow contributions" to this story.

—WFN

GETTING ALONG JUST FINE

Master morning in Bend, Oregon, almost four weeks into spring.

It was snowing outside his apartment again.

November, December, January, February, March, and now mid-April. Five and a half months of rain, wind and snow.

Frank hated rain, wind and snow. He felt sorry for himself, secluded here—trapped in his living room—with his wife, Elizabeth, back in California; they had been married over thirty years—still on fine terms, still cared about each other, would never get divorced—but would never live together again, either. Success as an artist (which he excelled in) hadn't been enough; they found out the hard way that quality did not necessarily translate into riches, especially once one grew older, and the opportunities dried up like a puddle in the desert. Twelve consecutive years of heavy debt had stressed her to the point of near collapse—she needed her personal space.

So, he had volunteered to get out of her life; he left sunny California and moved to this dark two-bedroom apartment in the Pacific Northwest because he had a good friend here—Bill Singer—who collected his work. Bill had over a thousand pieces. Soon, however, he discovered that Singer was almost always on the road, and they saw each other only infrequently. True, he'd been over to Bill's house for dinner a couple of times over the last year and a half (his wife was sweet) but their interaction was far less than Frank had originally hoped for. *Not Bill's fault. Just the way the cookie crumbled.*

At his age, it wasn't easy making new friends. Frank had lived in various parts of Greater Los Angeles for more than fifty years, and, although he wasn't a native, he felt that it was his true home. Not Missouri where he'd been born and raised, and certainly not Oregon where people liked to ski and hike and fish and climb mountains. He did none of these things. In Bend, he passed the time reading (classics he'd missed when younger, plus a hundred Max Brand Westerns), painting, watching television (reality shows, mainly) and sleeping—a *lot*: nine hours a night, plus another hour each afternoon.

Sure, he'd made a couple of new friends (both much younger) during his exile in Oregon, but they lived in Vancouver, Washington, a good distance from lonely, cold Bend. *There are always the pen pals*, he supposed. Sometimes he just liked to whine; truth be known, the complaining made the solitude more bearable.

Although Central Oregon was beautiful—ringed by the white-capped Cascade mountain range and thicketed with endless conifer trees—the beauty of nature didn't raise excitement in him; Frank preferred the agitation of a metropolis, with plenty of bookstores, theaters, all-night diners—even its car-choked freeways. Fired with a sense of constant motion, of existence lived at a heightened level, cities made him feel *more* connected to the world, while—paradoxically—the "great outdoors" made him withdrawn, sad, isolated; as though smothered in the bosom of its grandeur.

Bend was quiet; the silence was staggering. Tranquil to a fault. He was a latter-day Robinson Crusoe, except for the numbing cold. He planned a move to Tucson, Arizona next spring, for the heat if for no other reason. *I'd rather deal with the dry desert heat over the penetrating Oregon cold any day.* The gusty winds in Bend cut into his skin no matter what coat he wore. Even with the sun out, the winds were fierce.

Now it was late afternoon. *Still snowing. How long have I been standing here, daydreaming?* Frank moved to his bedroom, watching the awful snow feather down into the slushy street beyond the frosted glass of his window, flocking the trees. He was warming himself in front of the paltry wall heater when the phone rang. He walked into the second bedroom (converted into his studio) and picked up the receiver.

"Hello?"

"Hello, Frank. It's Charles."

"Oh, hi," said Frank. Charles was a frustrated producer living in California who was attempting to get a TV series off the ground. He wanted Frank to design the show's logo. *If and when…*

"I just talked to Eddie's wife, Shirley," he told Frank. "She asked about you, about how you were doing."

"I'm fine. Getting along just fine."

"Eddie is still very shaky after the stroke."

"Stroke! My God, when did that happen?"

"Couple of months ago. Eddie was driving in the San Fernando Valley when the stroke hit him; got into a minor accident, but nobody was hurt. Shirley says he's doing okay now. Can't drive anymore of course… The two of them, they just stay home in their apartment. Eddie never answers the phone. Doesn't want to talk to anybody. It's sad, really… "

"Well, I can understand that." There was a pause. Frank felt out of the loop; captivated by the snow in his view from the studio window as it hissed into the trees at the edge of the small apartment complex. It swallowed reality in a mantle of bluish-white, adding inches by the hour to an already deep accumulation. *Why did I ever come to Bend? Bend sucks!*

Frank's reflections and what his mother said when she was in her late seventies (as he now was) tumbled through his mind like the snow cascading to the frozen earth: *"If you live long enough you outlast your family and all of your friends—and unless you've had children you end up all alone in the world."*

He had never been a father.

As for his mother: she'd been right.

Indeed, he had outlasted his family (except for a first cousin—in his nineties—who resided in Santa Barbara) and most of his old friends: the brilliant Chuck, his best pal for over a decade, had aged seemingly overnight, a victim of early Alzheimer's disease. He died looking like an old man of ninety while still in his thirties… *Chuck's lovely wife, Helen, followed him to the grave four years later, of cancer (was it the stress of watching Chuck disintegrate that brought it on?)… Chad, my Texas friend, succumbed to melanoma… Paul died of acute diabetes in New York… Wendl suffered a fatal heart attack in Arizona… Pipes drowned inside the cabin of a commercial airliner after a crash out of Washington, DC… Bruce hanged himself somewhere in Oklahoma (just as his father had), following a severe bout of depression…*

Then there was Rod: he hadn't survived the open-heart surgery undertaken to save his life, in California, and Relling ended his life in a garage full of carbon monoxide… Squires lost his battle with lymphoma… Bob in Santa Barbara—bedridden after back surgery—never recovered… Dan (a real powerhouse of energy) and his wife Elaine both died of brain tumors… Dan's daughter, Linda, had preceded them in death: stoned on angel dust, she believed she could fly and jumped from the top of a ten-story building—she had been only twenty (I sense Dan never got over this, though we never spoke of the incident after the funeral)…

So many…

"Frank? Are you okay?" Charles asked, interrupting his thoughts. The cordless phone was old, the line prone to static. It was suddenly heavy in the aged man's fingers.

"I-I'm fine Charles… Sorry, what else is going on? How is the show coming along?"

"Glad you asked: there's been a little news… "

Frank listened, but really couldn't focus on Charles… His voice droned from the earpiece, blending into the wind gusts outside as the snow swirled like ash from Mt. St. Helens. He could feel the frigid air on his delicate skin as it permeated the thin glass of the old apartment window. *McKnight was hit by a car in Kansas City just after high school… my old school buddy, Bill Hennessey, survived a colon operation only to die five weeks later—ironically—of peritonitis, the same thing that killed my beloved father… Maggie—a chain-smoker who was never without a cigarette—died of lung cancer, the same way my old friend Stan lost his wife… Steve was unable to beat mesothelioma… Ken died in a fiery racing crash at Riverside and Arthur cut his throat after shooting his wife, Adele, back in Missouri (they had been like a second set of parents to me when I was a boy)… Jerry passed away after a series of strokes… OCee had some kind of deadly back problem… Phil died of Parkinson's… Back in K.C., Mary Kay's heart gave out… And Peter died suddenly in the U.K. while playing outside with his kids…*

Gone… All of them… Gone…

Well, it's like they say about life: nobody gets out alive. Frank's thoughts flashed suddenly to the vast multitude of soldiers—blue and gray—who perished in the Civil War. *The irony is, they'd all be dead by now even if there had never* been *a war!*

Friends, lovers, strangers—each as individual as a snowflake, each equally fragile, equally ephemeral. Here, then gone…

So many gone.

Even the few old friends I have left are in poor shape: Ray is a shadow of his former self—rendered half blind and half deaf (plus crippled in one leg) after his stroke at age 79… Dick is incredibly frail after those two spinal operations… Dennis, another chain smoker, with his tic and cigarette cough… Ada Beth, unable to walk, languishing in some rest home… and Herb, wracked with a variety of ills…

"Well, I can tell you're busy, Frank… How 'bout we chat next week, okay?" Charles offered at last, nervous as ever. Frank smiled, eyes rimmed in tears, brimming with remembrance and lament. *Where has all the time gone?*

"Sorry, Charles; I'm not much company right now! Next week will be fine; bye-bye." He hung the phone up without looking, still transfixed by the snowflakes' suicidal dance in the icy twilight, their lives at an end. *Where did all the time go?*

Overall, though, Frank had to admit that he had great family genetics: his father was close to eighty-eight when he died, his mother nearly eighty-five. His grandparents had both lived into their nineties, as did several aunts and uncles. Still, he couldn't depend on genetics alone for a longer life. *You make your own luck.* He worked out with weights, exercised on a trampoline, and took several vitamins and food supplements (zinc, pine bark, grape seed,and magnesium among others). He had never smoked, and had given up meat and coffee many years ago. Beyond a glass of wine now and then, he never drank alcohol. Soy products formed the basis of his vegetarian diet.

Result: I look, act and feel much younger than my calendar years.

Thinking about all of his dead family and friends as he watched the snow come down in the early evening chill, Frank was suddenly ashamed of feeling sorry for himself. *Dammit, I'm as healthy as a horse!*

That was a great blessing. A rare gift, especially at his age. *Like a beautiful snowfall, and the time and patience to enjoy it.* He smiled, now at ease with his thoughts, his memories, his apparitions: *To hell with self-pity.* He turned away from the window at last, picking up his paint brush and studying the abandoned landscape he had begun so long ago in California.

"By God, *I'm* alive …

and getting along just fine … "

Bill and I wrote this one together, taking turns as the characters in a notepad, trading reactions back and forth in real time. I was intrigued with the notion of two individuals discussing an event from differing perspectives, with completely opposite motivations. The e-mail presentation, I think, adds a layer of remove, a layer of realism. Terrible things happen to good people all the time: this is just another example…

—JVB

EXCHANGE
(with Jason V Brock)

Feed: GNews Wire—Local
Posted On: Sunday, March 13, 2011 10:03 PM
Author: News Alert (Police Watch)
Subject: BREAKING NEWS—Woman Found Murdered in Home

A woman in her early thirties was found dead in her home in the SW blocks of 137th Street this evening by Washington County deputies. Her identity is being withheld pending notification of relatives. Police were unable to release details about her death, but confirm that the case is being investigated as a homicide, and that they are looking for several persons of Interest based on evidence gathered at the crime scene…

From: RepublicOfReptiles@hotmail.com
Sent: Sunday, March 13, 2011 6:18 PM
To: IRONMAN1487@gmail.com
Subject: Help…

Something's happened. You've got to help me.

I walked into the house just a little while ago and there she was—already dead. I swear that's what happened! You know I love Erin: I would never want to hurt her!

I'm on the run; I panicked and left... I know I should've just gone to the cops, but I have my reasons for not trusting them (long story).

That's why I need your help: I've got to clear this up, fast. I think I know what happened—but I need your word that you won't tell anybody what's going on... You're the only person I can trust anymore!

Can you help me out?

~SJ

From: IRONMAN1487@gmail.com
Sent: Sunday, March 13, 2011 6:47 PM
To: RepublicOfReptiles@hotmail.com
Subject: RE: Help...
Wow! Erin's *dead*? *WTF??*

Okay, I'll help all I can. You can stay at my place until you figure out what to do next. Also, you could give the cops any tips anonymously: Don't give them your name, and make it a quick call so it can't be traced, or maybe use your cell.

Tell me where and when to meet you. I've got your back.

—F.E.

From: RepublicOfReptiles@hotmail.com
Sent: Sunday, March 13, 2011 7:03 PM
To: IRONMAN1487@gmail.com
Subject: RE: Help...
Thanks, man. I needed that...

We have to be really careful: Cops are probably going to be watching everybody I know, including you, Chuck, George… Right now, I'm hopping from Starbucks to Kinko's to wherever I can get free Wi-Fi. I've got my car, some clothes, my laptop and a little bit in the bank, but they might try to cut me off…

I mean, everything was OK at her house: no evidence of a break-in, no overturned furniture; I even had to unlock the door with the key she'd given me last week… Dinner was on the table, still warm. The minute I walked into the kitchen, though, I knew it was bad. And when I saw her… who would have done this to Erin?! I mean, she was all cut up, bloody—God! I had a feeling the cops might come after me, so I called in sick at work for tomorrow. When my new boss asked me why because I seemed fine just a couple of hours ago, I freaked and hung up on him: that job's probably shot.

I need cash—think you can help there? Just for a little while, until I can figure this out?

How could this happen to us?!

~SJ

From: IRONMAN1487@gmail.com
Sent: Sunday, March 13, 2011 7:31 PM
To: RepublicOfReptiles@hotmail.com
Subject: RE: Help…
I feel you, SJ. This is horrible!

Regarding funds: I'm a bit tight myself right now, but I could loan you a couple hundred bucks. Have to go on a trip this week.

As to why it happened: man, I can't answer that one… Maybe she was having an affair? What about Chuck? He used to talk about her boobs a lot, I remember. Told me he had a thing for her. George said they went out, too, before you guys met (not sure if you knew that, but might be valuable in this situation).

Anyway, maybe one of them was over and tried to make a move on her and things got out of hand. George *does* have a record for battery. Maybe we should look in that direction. Just a thought…

What do you plan to do now? You should really think about contacting the police!

—F.E.

From: RepublicOfReptiles@hotmail.com
Sent: Sunday, March 13, 2011 8:02 PM
To: IRONMAN1487@gmail.com
Subject: RE: Help…
No! She wasn't having any affairs… Didn't know that about Erin and George: well, everybody's got their skeletons, I guess. I know I do… Maybe it was just random, but still: no signs of a break-in. I could have missed something, though…

I CAN'T GO TO THE COPS! Not yet, anyway, not without some evidence that I didn't have anything to do with this… I guess I need to explain something here:

When I was a kid, I killed someone.

A girl: Theresa. Theresa Gurion. She was a nice girl… Something she did, though, it upset me.

Anyway, when I was about thirteen, I took a shotgun from my Grandfather's place and stashed it in my treehouse. I used to hang out there all the time, trying to escape Gramps and his rages. He'd become a real lush after Mom and Dad were killed in the accident. He screamed at Grandmother (rest her soul) and me almost daily… Beat us sometimes with his belt... It was a horrible time in my life...

Well, one day I invited Theresa to the house. I had a big crush on her. After school, she dropped by and I took her over to the treehouse after chores were done... Inside, we talked awhile, and started kissing; I began to touch her... She told me to stop, but I didn't; she felt too good to stop. I guess I got carried away, so I kept on, and she started screaming... We were a good distance from the house, and it was a pretty rural area in Arkansas anyway.

Her screaming—that made me really upset. She finally kicked away from me, got herself together. She was crying, yelling at me. I felt sick, ashamed, but also... enraged. So, as she was climbing down I got the gun from its hiding place, and... I shot her.

She died right there... When they came looking for us that evening, I was just sitting with her body, holding her.

I was ordered into a treatment program for young offenders. As part of my juvenile rehab, I had to learn to control my anger. I did; I HAVE. They sealed my juvie records—but it might be an issue if they tried to say I killed Erin, I don't know.

Help me! I didn't DO this!

~SJ

From: IRONMAN1487@gmail.com
Sent: Sunday, March 13, 2011 8:21 PM
To: RepublicOfReptiles@hotmail.com
Subject: RE: Help...
That. Is. Fucking. Crazy.

I mean, I don't know what to say! I didn't know about the treehouse girl. All these years, and you *never mentioned it*! WTF?? Shit, man: I *thought* I was your best friend! No secrets between us ... Well, it is what it is; guess I know you a little better now ...

All right: I have a new theory about Erin. Maybe she was back to being a heavy drinker, you know, in secret (she was off the sauce when we went out)? Do you think she could've been doing drugs behind your back or something?

Dude, maybe she offed herself. Did you check the body?

—F.E.

From: RepublicOfReptiles@hotmail.com
Sent: Sunday, March 13, 2011 8:49 PM
To: IRONMAN1487@gmail.com
Subject: RE: Help ...
We are best friends: I'm sorry I never told you about what I did—I just wanted to start over. That was so long ago ... A lifetime ago ...

Yes: I did check her body. What if I left my prints on it, though? God!

And Erin knew all about Theresa—but she still accepted me for ME.

Anyway, I've got money in the bank for about another week, provided they don't freeze my account or something. I could sure use that couple hundred in cash ...

~SJ

From: IRONMAN1487@gmail.com
Sent: Sunday, March 13, 2011 8:59 PM
To: RepublicOfReptiles@hotmail.com
Subject: RE: Help ...

First, I read somewhere that you can't get prints off human skin, so no problem there. Just tell me when you need the money, but I've got to catch a redeye tonight, so we need to meet up soon...

Also, I've had a new thought about this... you hit the booze fairly hard on occasion yourself (guess I know *why* now). I keep thinking about that night at Tony's in Chicago: you were really out of it, then didn't even remember it the next day.

Could it be that *you* had a blackout and did Erin in without being aware of what you were doing? Hey... it's >possible< right?

—F.E.

From: RepublicOfReptiles@hotmail.com
Sent: Sunday, March 13, 2011 9:21 PM
To: IRONMAN1487@gmail.com
Subject: RE: Help...
That's true—I've had my share of being pickled (in fact, I'm drinking more and enjoying it less daily), but no—we were supposed to go to a movie, then have some quiet time at home. I wasn't drinking.

I WAS running late at work, though, because of my new jerk boss; by the time I got home... **She was dead!**

I know that you've always cared about us—especially Erin: you'd want whoever did this to be caught.

Any money you can spare would be great! We have to be discreet, though...

Where? Downtown?

~SJ

From: IRONMAN1487@gmail.com
Sent: Sunday, March 13, 2011 9:30 PM
To: RepublicOfReptiles@hotmail.com
Subject: RE: Help …
Okay … let's say NO blackout. And I take it you don't agree about it maybe being Chuck or George.

No sign of a break-in *is* weird. So did she let someone in? That's a vital point. Maybe a salesman? A repairman? Could be someone she knew …

Best for me is my place. You know the address.

—F.E.

From: RepublicOfReptiles@hotmail.com
Sent: Sunday, March 13, 2011 9:42 PM
To: IRONMAN1487@gmail.com
Subject: RE: Help …
The only thing I know is that George never came over to her new place … Chuck has, but he's out of town for work this week. Repairman? Maybe, but I'm fairly handy, and Erin never mentioned needing anything done. Sales? On a Sunday? That seems sort of weird …

You know … It occurs to me that YOU had the only spare key—for when we go on vacation.

And … You never really got past Erin going out with me—did you? Man, I never meant that to transpire like it did: I just happened to be there when she broke up with you—it wasn't personal!

Maybe we need to stop e-mailing. I'll figure it out on my own.

~SJ

From: IRONMAN1487@gmail.com

Sent: Sunday, March 13, 2011 10:02 PM
To: RepublicOfReptiles@hotmail.com
Subject: RE: Help...
Sure, I have a spare key, but I've never used it. Boy, you're getting paranoid!

Why drag *me* into this mess of yours more than you already have?! Our breakup had nothing to do with you: It was strictly between us.

Better try and get your head on straight.

—F.E.

From: RepublicOfReptiles@hotmail.com
Sent: Sunday, March 13, 2011 10:03 PM
To: IRONMAN1487@gmail.com
Subject: RE: Help...
Right. Keep in touch!

~SJ

From: IRONMAN1487@gmail.com
Sent: Sunday, March 13, 2011 10:08 PM
To: RepublicOfReptiles@hotmail.com
Subject: RE: Help...
Cool it, man! You cutting me off is *not* going to solve your problems.

Look: Come over to my apartment and let's talk this through. Just park a block or two away and use the back stairs. The cops won't spot you even if they *do* start watching my building.

—F.E.

From: RepublicOfReptiles@hotmail.com
Sent: Sunday, March 13, 2011 10:13 PM
To: IRONMAN1487@gmail.com

Subject: RE: Help . . .

-OK-

Can you loan me the money? Three hundred?

~SJ

From: IRONMAN1487@gmail.com
Sent: Sunday, March 13, 2011 10:23 PM
To: RepublicOfReptiles@hotmail.com
Subject: RE: Help . . .

I said *two*. That's all I can spare; get yourself together! You're in deep shit, my friend.

Better keep it together, man. *Cool heads prevail.*

I mean, you've got no place to go . . . very little money . . . you just left the scene of a shooting . . . your fiancée has been murdered . . . You've got some *serious* problems to deal with here. And, to top it off, you've got that whole juvie record: Sealed or not, they'll try to hang it all on *you*, bro. Erin should have listened to me: maybe could have avoided all this BS . . .

Anyway: too late now.

I hope we can work this thing out together. I have to leave by midnight. Your move.

—F.E.

From: RepublicOfReptiles@hotmail.com
Sent: Sunday, March 13, 2011 10:37 PM
To: IRONMAN1487@gmail.com
Subject: RE: Help . . .

I never mentioned that she was >shot< as well as stabbed . . . Shot in the face.

How did you know that? I'll see you at your place in an hour: Be there. And get ready . . .

~SJ

Feed: GNews Wire—Local
Posted On: Monday, March 14, 2011 05:57 AM
Author: News Alert (Police Watch)
Subject: Two Men Found Dead in SW Apartment

Two males, both in their thirties, were found deceased early this morning in an apartment at the Russell Arms near 95th and Olympic. Both died of gunshot wounds, and the police suspect an apparent struggle over a semi-automatic weapon found at the scene to be the cause. It does not appear drug-related.

The bodies have not yet been identified.

Elly is not of this world. She's stuck here on Earth and is doing her level best to adapt. She seems nice enough, but has a disturbing habit of wanting to "see inside."

—WFN

MY GIRL NAME IS ELLY

Leonard: From high school. He's sixteen and he thinks he's my boyfriend, but no one is. Leonard acts like he's much older than me. Kind of stuck on himself. I'm sixteen too, which is not old. Or maybe I'm sixteen hundred. *That's* old, but I look like sixteen, not sixteen hundred. Leonard wears buckle boots like a girl, and shiny leather pants. With skulls painted on them. Leonard likes skulls. And he always combs his hair so that a lock of it falls across his forehead. He says Hitler did that, combed his hair that way. Does he like Hitler? Maybe he's a Nazi, but they don't have those anymore so far as I know. They have skinheads but not Nazis. Who would want to do anything Hitler did? He married Eva Braun (think that's how you spell her name) in the underground bunker when the Russians were taking over Berlin. Not much left to take over if you ask me. Just a lot of bombed-out buildings. I've seen pictures of them, all bombed out. Nobody could live in them anymore. Who would want to? Leonard is boring, actually. With his Hitler hair and skull pants. But he's okay for the kind of sex they have here.

Earth: What a funny planet to end up on. But maybe I won't end up here. Maybe I'll go on to other planets and open people on them like I do on this one. I tear people open because I like to see what's inside. I guess it's not a good thing to do, tearing people open, but I like doing it. Like shoplifting. Fun going to the mall with my friend Betty and stealing different stuff. Like gloves and combs and lipstick. Small stuff. You can get caught stealing big stuff like I did once when a store detective, Mister Sunny, saw me steal a nice coat with red silk lining. I tore him open and carried him into a storage closet. I'm very strong, a lot stronger than I look for a sixteen-year-old girl. I had to break Mister Sunny's neck to keep him from hollering. Boy, I would have been in bad trouble if any of the lady sales clerks had seen me break his neck. That store detective was the first Earth person that I opened up. When I tore him open he was comical inside with all of his white bones, goopy muscles and big red heart, red as a clown's nose. Clowns are neat, like when my planet mother took me to a circus.

Mother: She's maybe forty-five years old with shifty eyes and of course not my *real* mother. My real mom is far away on another planet where they have plant things like me who enjoy looking inside people or would if they were here to do it. (Yeah, I'm a plant thing. Big deal!) Mother—this Earth one—has short, stumpy legs and real slitty lips, like they aren't there at all; like closed purse strings. She's super religious. Goes to some crappy church each Sunday and wears a dumb hat with a veil. I'd never wear a dumb hat like that. She smokes a ton of cigarettes that make her teeth yellow like old piano keys, and her breath stinks. She doesn't like me and calls me a slutty bitch. But I'm officially adopted so she's stuck with me. She thinks I'm ugly. Ha! She should see what I *really* look like, all green and lumpy with purple roots. When I got to this planet I fixed myself to look like other young girls with a snub nose and lots of freckles—like Betty looks only better. She's dumpy like mother and her hair is stringy. And she uses too much lipstick. And too much perfume. But maybe she'd smell bad if she didn't. She probably has funny insides and someday I'll open her up and find out.

Father: He's maybe fifty or so. Thick glasses. Mostly bald. Got an ulcer. Drives one of those big rigs with all the wheels across country so he/s not home much which is okay with me because we don't get along much. He had a favorite dog, Arnold, a pit bull, and mean. Real mean. Barked all the time. Chased cars. Bit two little kids on Halloween. (Father settled out of court.) I'd never seen what's inside a mean dog like Arnold before I opened him up and father figured I was responsible for Arnold's just vanishing the way he did. Which was true but I denied it. I'm no dummy. You can talk to animals (although they sure look different) where I come from and after they answer you back. I told Arnold to stop biting people, after he tried to bite me is when I opened him up to look inside. He was sort of interesting in there but not as interesting as people are. Anyhow Father and I are at "logger hogs." That's what he says we are at. He gets Earth words mixed up like that sometimes. So that's father for you.

Me: I look in the mirror and I have to laugh when I do because I don't look like me at all. For one thing I have a lot more teeth as a spiny plant and I don't have what Earth girls call "boobies." They're pretty big, the ones I have, and I wear a harness for them called a bra which is real hot in summer and makes them all sweaty. Where I come from we don't have boobies and we don't sweat. But you take what you get and summer just lasts three months, with only one real hot one, so it's okay to have boobies and sweat.

Santa: I'm generally disappointed when I open people up. Guess I'm getting jaded; it's lost a lot of charm for me. At Christmas, in the mall, I met Santa Claus in a storage room (he wanted to see my boobies) and opened him up. Thought he'd be full of snow and jingle bells and holiday tinsel, but he wasn't. Just the same old ribs and gooey red stuff. It was what Betty calls a "bummer." Earth people never seem to be full of fun stuff.

Lovecroft: A guy named H.P. Lovecroft (is that how you spell him?) wrote a lot of stuff I read in high school about big slimy things with tentacles (what are those?) who live deep in the Earth and give people a real hard time. They sound like fun. I'd like to meet one sometime to see what's inside. But I guessI never will. Bummer.

Home: Well, first of all, I'm not some kind of space nerd who hops around to different planets and all. I've only been to four planets so far: Mars, for a picnic a long time ago (bor-ing!) Jupiter, to one of its moons (forget which one) my home, Itchim (of course), and to where I am now, Earth. That's actually just three planets and a moon. My home is not close to this galaxy. It's way off so far your head would swim just thinking about it. So … you ask, *just how in heck did I get here to Earth*? Well, I popped through a "worm hole" (and if you don't know what one is, that's your problem). I landed here by mistake. Was headed somewhere else—to a planet named Gupper, which means "happy fish." Anyhow, being here, I decided to become an Earth girl and got adopted by my dumpy mother and bald father who wanted a kid but were sterile. By the way, my girl name is Elly. Sweet, huh? That was four Earth years ago. About three seconds in Itchim time.

As for me opening people up to see what's inside, I just do that when I'm bored. And I get bored real easy. I opened up a postal worker named Bob last month, thinking maybe he'd be full of letters, but he just had bones and stuff. Another bummer. I'm amazed to find that Earth people cook and eat quite a number of their animals: pigs, cows, chickens, turkeys and birds. I talked to some of them, the animals, and a pig told me they call him "bacon" which is a cover name for dead pig. In China, they even eat dogs and cats. If Father had lived in China he might have eaten Arnold. A turkey told me they were going to eat him for Thanksgiving. On my planet, we don't eat our animals. We eat trees and bushes. (Mighty tasty!) I tried to eat an Earth tree but the bark was all hard and leaves got stuck in my teeth. Maybe if I can find another worm hole I'll go back home where things make sense. But worm holes are tough to find.

High School: Wow! High school is where I go like the other sixteen-year-olds because you have to. All the boys like my boobies, but the teachers are all glum-faced old poops (That's what Betty calls them). One old poop, Mister Vincent, keeps getting my girl name wrong. Calls me Nellie instead of Elly, but that's okay. Sometime I'll open him up to see if he's full of books. High school has lots of yelling, dopey, dumb-ass kids, but it's where I learned about how Hitler combed his hair.

Father again: I got bored playing TV games last weekend and decided to open up Father. He was back from a truck drive to Seattle and was in the living room reading the paper when I told him I was going to open him up. (I hoped to find a truck tire inside him). What in hell are you talking about he asked me and I just smiled and tore him open. Fooey! Same ole stuff. That's when Mother came in from the kitchen and said *real loud* "Oh my God! Oh my God, you crazy little bitch! What have you done to Dennis?" (That was father's name.) "He's boring inside," I told her, and she had me arrested. And now I'm in a cell at the Juvenile Detention Center where I'm writing all this crap down.

Archie: There's a big-belly fat guard who brings me Earth food named Archie. And next time he comes along with Earth food (I really miss eating trees!) I intend to pull off my cell door (I told you I'm very strong) and open up Archie. I've never seen inside a jelly belly.

Should be fun.

I have always been fascinated by the spectacular rise and sad decline of the eccentric billionaire Howard Hughes. Business tycoon… playboy… movie mogul… aviator… inventor… he was an iconic figure of the 20th Century. Having read several books about him, my interest grew. Thus, the character of Bernard Fielding in "The Recluse" is very clearly based on the late Howard Hughes. No writer could ask for better dramatic material.

Of course, my duo of nosy reporters, Vince Evans and Ellen Burns, are totally my invention—and what Vince uncovers is strictly from my imagination.

I wonder what Hughes would think of it all if he were still living? He probably wouldn't give a damn!

Enough said. My story awaits you.

—WFN

THE RECLUSE

The train depot in Tucson, Arizona.

Very early morning, with the sun just edging the eastern horizon. Night shadows linger as the Arizona sky is gradually stained with pink light.

A train rolls to a stop, its engine pulling a single passenger coach. The coach windows are covered by drawn curtains. A group of eager reporters, cameras at the ready, converge on the train as an ambulance backs up to the exit door of the coach. Cameras click and flash as a blanket-covered figure is carried from the train by two black-clad attendants and placed on a stretcher inside the vehicle.

Once the ambulance doors are closed, one of the attendants steps up to the forest of microphones on the train platform. The reporters press forward, a hush falling on the crowd.

"Mr. Fielding will henceforth be controlling his business interests from new headquarters at the Royal Sierra Hotel here in Tucson. Mr. Fielding asks that his privacy be respected."

Refusing to take questions, the speaker retires to the ambulance, which then glides away into the shadowed morning.

By noon, the Internet is alive with news of Fielding's latest move. CNN anchor Leiland Cooper announces: "Bernard F. Fielding has taken over the entire penthouse floor of the Royal Sierra Hotel here in Tucson. The reclusive business mogul, owner of several film studios and global corporations, as well as Fielding Aviation, has not made a public appearance for more than a decade. The legendary multi-billionaire conducts all of his financial affairs through his business partner, Nelson Mayhew. The eccentric Fielding is now—"

In his Hollywood apartment, Vincent Evans switches off the television, leaning back in a recliner, his hands tented. He's in his early thirties, lean, desert-tanned and muscular.

"Eccentric is *right*," he says to Ellen Burns, as she adds more Zinfandel to her empty glass. "I consider myself a damn clever investigative report, but every time I try to reach Fielding I get a door slammed in my face."

"So *you're* the hotshot reporter," mocks Ellen, sipping the wine. "What am *I*, chopped liver?" She is blonde, in her twenties, with a lush body firmed by daily gym sessions. "I've been trying to reach Fielding myself for ages," she says. "How *old* is this guy by now anyway?" Her brow furrows in unconscious revulsion.

Vince chuckles, turning in the chair. "Who knows? Every bio I've seen has him born in a different year," he replies. He studies her for a moment, then looks back at his hands.

She nods. "At least we know he signs contracts ... talks on the phone ... " She trails off, lifting the wine glass to her lips.

"I hear tell even his goon squad never sees him in person," Vince says.

"No, that can't be true," she replies. "They take care of him, bring him food, the whole bit."

"The way I hear it," Vince continues, "the food is put

outside his door. When they leave he brings it in and whenever he travels he keeps his face and body totally covered."

"But why?" she asks. "When he was young, he was seen out on the town with every woman in Hollywood. He had girlfriends stashed in apartments all over town." She takes another sip.

Vince regards her again, turning in the chair. He shrugs, then says: "And as an aviator, he had his picture in all the papers. He even appeared at a Senate hearing in Washington regarding his purchase of Global Airlines. Then … nothing. No interviews, no photos, nada. What happened to change him?"

"Could've been Mona, that ex-showgirl he married … the one they called The Body," says Ellen. "Marriage can affect a big change in a man. I interviewed her for *Newsweek* when Fielding was named Man of the Year."

"I remember," Vince replies. "He had his face on the cover."

"That was before he got involved in building that crazy super-plane for the government," she says. "Far as I know it's still sitting there in the Arizona desert. Never even had a test flight. He keeps it under a tight guard. My bet is it'll never get off the ground."

He pauses, then: "Incidentally, I read your *Newsweek* interview with Mona. She seemed like a cold one."

"Oh, she was one cold bitch," Ellen agrees. "And she sure didn't express much love for hubby."

He nods. "But she loved his money. Must've pissed her off when his will was made public and she found out where all the dough is going once he kicks … To a bunch of weird animal charities. Doesn't leave her her a cent."

"You can buy a lot of pet food for his kind of money." She smiles. "After the *Newsweek* thing, they split up. His lawyers made sure that Mona got nothing out of him. Yet I hear she's living the good life in Monaco. Has her own yacht, a new Mercedes, a fancy apartment in Monte Carlo full of antique furniture . . . "

Vince looks up. "Who's footing the bill?"

"Beats me," she replies.

He shrugs, tipping the wine bottle to refill his glass.

"It was after the split," she continues, "that Fielding became a recluse. Shut himself off from the world. It's like he wants to disappear. No photos. No face-to-face interviews. *Why?*"

Vince shakes his head. "Maybe he doesn't like the idea of people seeing him get old. Could be vanity, my dear Ellen, sheer vanity."

"You know, somehow, I just don't buy that," she tells him. "I mean, think about it. I'm convinced there's something else behind all this. We need to keep digging."

He grins. "Maybe win a Pulitzer for the story of the century. I agree," he says. "We need to keep digging."

She checks her watch. "Wow, I didn't realize how late it is. Look, I've got to go feed my cat. Buster goes ape if he doesn't get his usual meal on time. Craps all over the kitchen floor." She finishes her wine, picking up her purse and slinging it over one shoulder. At the door, she turns back to face him. "You still plan to fly to Tucson this weekend?"

"You bet I do. I think Fielding's been playing a crooked game and I want to find out the truth."

"You'll never get into that penthouse," she declares. "You won't get within a mile of Fielding."

He nods. "Maybe I won't need to."

"You've got another plan?"

He smiles mysteriously. "Don't I always? Trust me on this."

“I’m going with you,” she says firmly.

“No dice, lady! I’m going stag on this one.” He grins at her.

“Hey! I want in on this story.”

He puts a hand up to quiet her. “You will be. Working as a team, I believe we can get the goods on the reclusive Mr. Fielding. I need you here, though.”

She pouts. “To do what?”

“To run down all the info on Fielding’s front man, Nelson Mayhew. Talk to people who know him. Nose around, find out what you can about him. I think he’s tied into something dark.”

She looks doubtful. “From what I hear, nobody will talk about Mayhew. He’s put out the word to keep mum or else. What makes you think they’ll talk to me?”

“Because you’re writing a bio on him. That makes you legit. I’ll provide an OK from Fielding under his personal signature.”

She arches an eyebrow. “Faked, of course.”

He grins. “Of course. You know I have a natural talent for forgery.”

“And what if they contact Fielding to verify the Mayhew bio?”

He spreads his hands. “They won’t. He’s unreachable.”

A week later, Vince receives a call from Ellen on his cell phone. “What’s happening?”

Her voice is strained. “*Nothing* is happening. I’m totally frustrated. Been beating the bushes for info on Mayhew—with zip results. Like chasing a ghost.”

“Were you able to locate people who know him?”

“Sure, but they wouldn’t talk. They treated me like a leper.”

"Maybe they didn't buy your story about doing a bio on him."

"No, that's not it. They've obviously been warned to clam up. People are afraid to talk about him. He's got some kind of *hold* on them."

"Blackmail?" he asks.

"Could be," she says. "He probably knows all their dark secrets. Mayhew's been in bed with a lot of shady characters over the years." She sighs. "Getting inside info on him is *impossible.* It's like hitting a brick wall."

"Ummm ... " Vince ponders her words. "Well ... at least you gave it a good shot."

"I'm sorry," she says, regret in her tone. "What about *your* plan?"

"It's still on."

"And you're not gonna try to reach Fielding?"

"Like I said, I don't need to."

Her voice is tinged with doubt. "Be careful, Vince. I have a bad feeling about all this. Woman's intuition."

"Don't worry," he assures her. "I'll be fine."

"Promise to let me know how things go?"

"I promise," he says. "There is an old Native American saying: 'If you wish to enter the eagle's nest, you must wear his feathers.'"

"What's that mean?"

"It means I intend to have a closer look at The Titan—and I'll be wearing the right feathers ... "

Late evening in the Arizona desert beyond Tucson, the sun's dry heat replaced by cold night air. A full moon rides the sky. Two of Fielding's security guards warm their hands at an open fire in front of the looming six-story hangar housing The Titan. They carry assault rifles and belted sidearms.

"How long does Fielding expect us to stay out here freezing our butts off?" the first guard asks.

"Shut your yap, Wilson," snaps the second guard. "With the money you're getting, you got no right to whine."

Wilson grunts, scratching his chin. "You've got a point *there*, Ben." He looks toward the hangar. "Think this bird's ever gonna fly?"

"That's not our concern," Ben replies. "That's up to the Boss. Fielding calls the shots."

"He's a real oddball... You never know what he's going to do next," mutters Wilson.

"We should be so odd. He's a freakin' *billionaire!*"

Wilson reacts to a pair of approaching headlights. "Looks like we got us some company."

A dusty service truck bearing the logo *Albright Inspections* brakes to a stop in front of the hangar. The uniformed driver exits the vehicle, walking up to them.

"Hello boys," says Vincent Evans. "My name is Rogers, and I've been authorized to inspect The Titan."

"Authorized?" Wilson glares at him. "Just who the hell authorized you?"

"The old man himself." Evans shows Wilson a directive bearing the scrawled signature of Bernard Fielding. "No need for you boys to go inside with me. I just have to check out a couple of things. Shouldn't take me long."

Wilson looks skeptical. "Well...," he hesitates a moment, suspicion clouding his features. "Fielding never told us about you, *Rogers*."

"He never tells anyone about anything," says Vince. "Unlock the door."

"Okay," says Wilson, nodding toward Ben. "Let him in."

Ben produces a ring of keys, opening the entry door for Vince.

He smiles at them before stepping inside the cavernous hangar.

The Titan, striped by moonlight from overhead vents, is a modern marvel, filling the vast interior of the building. Evans knows the statistics, but the actual reality is stunning. The giant aircraft is five stories tall and longer than a city block, with a wingspan of three hundred and twenty feet. From its eight radial engines, four along each wing, The Titan boasts a combined thrust of 40,000 horsepower, and able to achieve a cruising speed of 300 miles an hour over a 3,000-mile range. Constructed from laminated birchwood, it is the largest airship in history, designed to seat some eight hundred passengers.

Vince crosses over to the huge plane, climbs into the hull, and enters the ship's interior.

Where are the seats? The vast fuselage is an empty shell.

Vince goes to the cockpit, settling into the padded pilot seat to check out the massive instrument panel. *Fake!* The façade is most impressive, but behind the instruments themselves, Vince uncovers a tangle of loose wiring. *Damn! Is the whole* thing *a scam?*

He exits the plane, moving to the engines. Atop a steel ladder at engine one, Vince uses a screwdriver to remove the engine cowling and finds just what he expects—an empty shell. *Fake, all of it, fake!*

Slipping out his cell phone, he takes several photos of the engine's empty interior. Vince quickly descends the ladder to face the barrel of Wilson's assault rifle.

"Well, *Rogers,* how was your little photo session?" Wilson's tone is cold.

Vince shrugs. "It was great until you showed up."

Wilson jerks the rifle barrel in the direction of the exit door. "Get moving," he commands. Vince complies before abruptly chopping the rifle barrel aside, running from the hangar as the guards give chase.

"Grab him, Ben!" shouts Wilson. "Don't let him get away!"

Vince dodges past Ben, sprinting for the truck. He is unable to get the truck door open before Ben tackles him. As they fall to the ground, Vince fumbles with the cell phone, but it escapes his grip.

Wilson rushes up. "Can't have *that*," he snaps, smashing the phone under his booted heel. "I ran your truck logo on the office Internet. There's no such company as *Albright Inspections*. You're a goddamn phony! Get your damn hands up!"

Evans complies, raising both arms. "So now what?"

"Now you go beddy-bye," snarls Wilson, slamming the barrel of the rifle across Evans' skull.

A swirl of brightness. A ripple of shifting images. Wavering figures.

Vince Evans blinks rapidly, his eyes achieving clear focus. Three bulked figures are standing over him. One of them holds a .45 automatic. He's tall with a white brush mustache masking a scarred harelip. He wears a smartly tailored gray suit and sports a large emerald ring on his right hand. Evans recognizes him from a hundred media photos: Nelson Mayhew.

His .45 is pointed at Evans.

"Get him up!" Mayhew orders the other two men, large-bodied with pale emotionless faces. "Get him up!" Mayhew orders the other two men, large-bodied with pale emotionless faces. Projecting an aura of raw menace, they roughly lift Evans to a standing position. His wrists are taped behind his back and a thin ribbon of dried blood spirals down from his forehead.

"Where am I?" Evans asks, squinting against the brightness of the room.

"Penthouse at the Sierra," snaps Mayhew.

Evans swallows, nods. "You're making a big mistake and you'll pay for it. Kidnapping is a damn serious offense."

Mayhew scoffs. "No one will ever know you were here," he says. Then, in a mock media-tone: "Investigative reporter disappears in desert." He smiles. "And that's where you'll end up—in a desert grave."

Vince is unfazed, attempting to loosen his wrists. "So you're going to kill me?"

"Do you actually *believe* we'd allow you to live with what you know about The Titan?"

"Yeah," nods Vince. "I know that Fielding Aviation ripped off the government for over a billion in development money. That plane was never meant to fly."

"Correct," says Mayhew. "But let's give credit where credit is due. The Titan scam was all *my* idea. Fielding had the connections, but I pulled off the deal. I'm a very clever fellow, after all."

Evans smiles thinly. "I don't doubt that, but you're just a front man for Fielding."

Mayhew stiffens, waving the gun as he steps forward. "Oh, I'm much more than that," he declares, agitated. "I know you've been stalling, but it doesn't matter—you're a dead man, Rogers. Or should I say *Evans*." Mayhew relaxes. "I've instructed my men to track down your partner, too. What's her name? Burns?" He smiles without humor. "They'll be sure to show her a good time."

Vince's eyes widen, trying to stay cool as he works his wrists. "Where is he? Where's Fielding?"

"In limbo." Mayhew chuckles. "Am I right, boys?"

The other two nod, remaining ominously silent.

Evans, in shock: "You've killed him?"

"Not entirely," says Mayhew.

"What kind of answer is that?"

"The only one you'll get," says Mayhew. "I think it's time to say goodbye, Mr. Evans. Your brief sojourn on Mother Earth is about to end."

"Beautifully phrased—for a murdering son-of-a-bitch."

"Feel free to indulge your penchant for insult," says Mayhew. "Sticks and stones may break my bones, but names … well, you know the rest."

"You're an unending source of wit."

Mayhew nods. "It's good to be appreciated." Then, in a harsh tone to the twin goons: "Enough idle chatter: Take Mr. Evans out to the desert and blow his head off."

As they move toward Vince, the door to the penthouse explodes inward and four uniformed officers, led by police lieutenant Malcolm Bradley storm into the room, guns drawn.

"Hands up!" orders Bradley. "Do it *now!*"

His order is obeyed.

Mayhew remains calm, turning to face Evans. "So you notified the police?"

"I didn't, but Ellen Burns obviously did. I texted her the photos of The Titan before your guard smashed my cell phone."

"How clever of you," nods Mayhew.

"Yes, like yourself, Mr. Mayhew, I'm also a very clever fellow."

Officer Bradley faces Mayhew. "Where's the big boy? Where's Mr. Fielding?"

"In the bedroom," Mayhew says. He leads them down a long hallway to a closed door. He gestures. "In there … But you might be surprised at what you find."

Fielding, stretched on the bed, looks far older than his

fifty-odd years: He is skeletal, eyes glazed, his cheeks deeply sunken, his matted hair spread out like a halo on the stained pillow. He tries to speak, but cannot, his mouth twisting with the effort.

Mayhew stands near the bed. "Technically, he should be dead. Had a major stroke ten years ago and would've died of it, but I found a way to keep him alive. His brain was the only part of him I cared about. He's a true genius, and that brain of his has made me a very rich man."

"So that's where Mona Fielding gets her money," Evans declares.

"Yes, we became lovers shortly before the *Newsweek* piece… Fielding found out about our relationship, and that's why they split. He was all set to fire me before the stroke hit him."

"And *after* the stroke," Evans prompts, "that's when you used Fielding to come up with the 'Titan' scam."

"Correct," says Mayhew. "That was only *one* of the ways I used him. Learned to fake his signature and voice on the phone. Of course, I couldn't let him be seen in public. People had to believe he was still able to function. And of course, in a way he *was*."

"Well now it's over," says Bradley. "Cuff him, boys, then get Mr. Fielding to a hospital. He's due for some tender loving care."

Mayhew is handcuffed and led away.

On the phone to Ellen, Vince fills her in on the full operation.

"It's quite a story," she says. "Think it'll win a Pulitzer?"

Vince grunts. "By golly, it just might," he says.

And they laugh together.

Richard Matheson's talented son, R.C., is noted for his bare-bones storytelling. His work is super-lean, with no wasted words. With "Dysfunctional," I asked myself: "Just how *lean can you get?" This is the result.*

—WFN

DYSFUNCTIONAL
(for R.C. Matheson)

Night.
Cold.
Wet streets.
Pale neons.
Bar.
Warm inside.
Whiskey.
Glow.
Ready for another.
Sexy blonde.
Alone at bar, smiling.
At him.
Knows he's attractive.
No problem with her.
Back to his place.
Laughing, holding his arm.
Inside.
Music on stereo.
Cozy.
Fire and champagne.
Pills into her glass.
Woozy, she tells him.

Like the others.
Really dizzy.
Tells her you'll be fine.
She stumbles.
Falls.
Knife.
Same one as before.
Uses it.
Blood.
Warm feeling.
Cuts up body.
Plastic bags.
To car.
Bags into river.
Back to bar.
Another tonight?
No, enough.
Tomorrow night.
Another then.
How many for the knife?
Lost count.
Dozens.
Back to apartment.
Father there.
Dysfunctional parent.
Sick-minded.
Has knife.
Stabs.
Blood in mouth.
Can't breathe.
Father laughs.
Dysfunctional.
Like father, like son.

Jason challenged me to write something outside my regular comfort zone, and said to keep it a non-genre story. I thought about it, and was able to come up with this. It's quite intense, but I really like it.

—WFN

DESCENT

It all concluded in amazing slow motion, but that was yet to come:

For now, he was sitting at his desk, hunched over the computer, fingers dancing at the keys; he had to complete the Tuesday report before the weekly ten o'clock staff meeting.

He was fifty-six and balding, taking prescription drugs for an enlarged prostate. He'd been working for Statler & Sons for two full decades and knew everyone by their first names. As a youngster, he'd earned straight As in Calculus and Physics. He had been no good at sports—self-conscious about his gawky, overweight frame and bad eyes—but had always been a real demon with numbers, calculations and theorems. The algebra of human interactions, however, had always been harder for him to grasp.

He was a widower, and had been for just over five years. His wife, Sally, had contracted breast cancer at fifty years of age, which eventually metastasized. Though she had both breasts removed, it wasn't enough to stop the disease. She died a year after the operation. Luckily, his health insurance had covered all costs. They had no children. In retrospect, he estimated that that was a blessing, though sometimes he wondered.

While he was not a religious man in any conventional sense, he did believe in God—he just wasn't sure Who (or What) God was (or wasn't). For that matter, he wasn't *exactly* sure where Heaven was (or wasn't) located.

He was a zealous worker, very loyal to the firm. No one had kept the books of Statler & Sons the way he kept them; everything was neat, every penny duly noted and accounted for; in all this time, he'd never made an error. In his dedication, he'd neglected his own enrichment: he'd never been much of anywhere, having grown up in the City. After Sally's death, he had leased a small one-bedroom apartment, usually walking to work. He'd never been to Europe, nor had he seen any of the other States. They had planned to, of course, but plans sometimes are derailed; out of the clear blue, other forces can totally change your destiny, it seems.

Someday, he promised himself, *I'll take that long vacation and "see the world," just like we always planned.* That was the phrase he used around his co-workers: "see the world." Secretly, he couldn't imagine just how he would be able to pay for such a vacation. There was no chance of familial assistance: his in-laws had never liked him, blaming him for Sally's decision not to pursue her legal career, and his parents—blue-collar factory folk—had never had any money to spare.

Actually, the idea of travel frightened him: strange places, foods, smells, a different language to comprehend. He had long ago established his own restricted comfort zone, and was loath to step beyond its boundaries. Foreign travel was merely a self-indulged fantasy. He believed in following a familiar routine; there was security in known ritual. *No risks.* He had never been a risk taker.

Recently, during his coffee breaks (although he never drank coffee), he found himself chatting more and more often with the newly hired secretary. Betty had been with Statler & Sons for just three months, a cute, pale-cheeked, mousey girl with a flat chest and watery gray eyes. When she smiled her eyes turned into slits, which he had to admit he found rather fascinating; she was mysterious.

"How do you like working for the firm?" he asked.

"Oh, I like it just fine. Mr. Statler is *such* a nice man!"

"He's very fair to his employees," he replied, nodding his head. "A nice man."

"Yes, he is," she agreed. He's very nice." Their conversation drifted into silence. She shifted in her chair, toying with her necklace. She smiled that smile. He blushed.

"Well, time for work," he said.

Back at his desk, he adjusted his bifocals and leaned forward, fingers poised over the computer keys as he tried to suppress his thoughts. He glanced at the clock on his desk. *Damn, I have to remember to vote today on my lunch hour...*

That was when he felt the concussion. The building shuddered and very soon streamers of dark smoke began to seep into the office.

"What was *that*?" the girl asked, rushing into his workspace.

"Some sort of explosion, sounded like; they were supposed to do some HVAC work on the other side of the building, maybe something happened... "

"Oh, dear; I hope no one's hurt...," she said, brow knit in concern.

"No way of telling," he said, "but I'm sure it's nothing to worry about. This is a very safe building. I doubt if anyone's been injured."

"But the smoke... it's getting thicker!"

Other workers in the room outside his office were muttering amongst themselves.

Betty glanced toward the exit door. "Maybe we should leave…"

"No, no…," he said, shaking his head. "Whatever the problem is, Maintenance will deal with it."

"But the smoke… it just keeps coming." Her concern was justified. The smoke was now billowing up from below in oily clouds, like a dark wash of ocean fog. She began to cough.

"Here, I'll get you some water; just have a seat and calm down, everything will be fine," he said, heading for the office cooler.

Upon his return, he noticed that it was getting hot inside the room. She gulped down the water as he removed his coat and loosened his tie. "Becoming quite warm in here," he observed.

"It's a fire!" she exclaimed, eyes panicked. "Things are burning. I can smell it!"

"Nothing serious," he assured her again. "They'll have it out in no time. You'll see."

The heat was increasing by the minute. Smoke was rapidly filling the office.

A kerchief to her mouth, the young woman was coughing violently. Her face was flushed, her eyes watering.

"Lie down," he advised, helping her. "Smoke rises. You'll be able to breathe better."

"Why doesn't it stop?" she gasped. "Why aren't they stopping it?"

He had no answer as he joined her on the floor. The acrid smoke fumes had turned his throat raw. It was difficult to swallow. The other employees were equally distressed. People were crying and screaming; a group of men huddled together in the middle of the office outside his door, gesticulating as they deliberated over what to do next.

He pulled the phone down from the desk above him. Holding the phone to his ear, he detected no dial tone; the line was dead. Instinctively, he drew the girl's shivering frame next to his: she was crying now.

"I'm going for the elevator!" She screamed, jumping up and running for the exit before he could reason with her. A few remaining employees quickly followed her: he never saw them again.

He recalled the red-lettered warning posted above the elevator: USE STAIRS IN CASE OF FIRE. DO NOT USE ELEVATORS.

Surely they would heed this warning and take the stairs down? Perhaps I'd better join them…A shame, though, to leave the office deserted… Important papers here. Yet, given the circumstances, Mr. Statler would understand… Mr. Statler was *a very nice man…*

His hesitation proved to be a grave mistake: the only exit suddenly bloomed into a wall of roaring flame.

Dear God, the fire's right here!

The cooler was behind him, so he used the water to soak his coat which he then wrapped around his head: it didn't help much.

Christ, I'm going to be burned alive!

He was forced to retreat to his office window as the furnace-hot flames rapidly advanced, eating their way across the office floor, devouring wood, plastic and paper. The flames had nearly reached him, the heat searing his skin. In desperation, he grabbed an office chair to smash out the glass pane, but it just bounced off the reinforced glass laminate. He tried again, and again, and a third time, to no avail. Summoning one last burst of adrenaline, he hammered the window a final time and the glass relented in a cyclone of air swooshing from the shattered portal.

He leaned out of the jagged window opening, squinting through the sooty fumes and waving his coat.

Someone will see me… Someone will come to save me…

But no one came for him; he was alone.

The fire was licking at his shoes now; his feet were blistering inside the leather.

He looked down for the first time, cringing at the sudden vertigo he experienced.

The flames were all around him. Black smoke choked his lungs. Tongues of fire began to devour his clothing. The left sleeve of his shirt was ablaze. The heat was unbearable, and he screamed in agony.

Then, he was aloft… *How can I survive a fall from this height?* This was a question that he refused to consider further.

He'd seen films of skydivers on television, how they seemed to float, effortlessly gliding on currents of air. That was how it seemed now, to him—that he was floating, feather-light, that it would take forever to reach the street so far below…

He had all the time in the world to think about his life, about all the magic places he'd never visited, never seen: Rome, with it's great Colosseum; London and Big Ben; Paris and the Eiffel Tower—the many states he'd read about—the Big Sky country of Montana; the flat wheat fields of Kansas; the Loop in Chicago; the high hills of San Francisco…

He was a virgin when he'd married Sally… God he missed her! He was ashamed of some things: she would gently chide him about his lack of sexual experience… Sex with his wife had been something less than successful… The Church had ruined him. He was tentative and afraid to let himself go, to lose himself in the sexual act… He had been a poor lover, but a good husband.

He wondered, now, falling past floor after floor, what sex

would have been like with other women. Perhaps he could have functioned better with other women. *Perhaps.*

Down and down… the windows of the other floors were blurred together, the screams of others barely audible over the incredible wind generated by his own clumsy flight… the street scene below was becoming clearer: he could see the crowds clustered like a colony of ants around the building. Lots of activity.

Fire trucks. Ambulances. Police cars. All for me…

Down and down… He could taste the fire wind, with the sweltering scent of flames burning his nostrils.

He discovered that he was suddenly not afraid to die. *Everyone dies. I might have lived to be a stoop-backed old man with gout and rheumatism and failing eyesight. Full of pain, unable to walk. This is better. Quick, decisive, painless…*

He thought about his father, who had suffered a stroke at seventy-nine: *Whole left side of his body useless. Blind in one eye. Unable to speak.*

And his mother: *Dead at sixty after suffering for ten years with rheumatoid arthritis. Life was a daily torture. She'd been forced to quit her factory job at fifty because of health problems. But she never showed her pain; she was one tough lady…*

No brothers or sisters. An only child. Spoiled and fussed over like a baby well into adulthood…

Down and down… *Just like the poor stewardess in Dickey's 'Falling'…*

Now the street below was coming up at him fast. That was how it seemed. He was floating, free and easy, but the street was coming up fast to meet him as he approached terminal velocity.

Fast…

The street coming up…

Me, waiting for it: suspended in Time and Space… Still,

permanent, unchanging, unmoving… the only known exception to Newton's Second Law of Motion… He smiled, tears evaporating instantly as he plummeted.

He was unexpectedly sorry to have failed Mr. Statler. *I'm in charge of keeping the books, of making sure that they are in perfect order…* Then he smiled; there were no books. *Not now.* The fire gobbled them up like a Polar Bear gulps down fish.

No books. All gone… He laughed, but the incredible wind stole the breath from his lungs.

He thought about God: *Is God watching me fall? If God wanted to, then (He or She) could just reach down from Heaven and catch me, like catching a baseball… But maybe God was too busy to notice my descent. Too busy with all the other billions of people that needed special care… Perhaps it slipped his notice, just this once… Does God sleep? Maybe he was napping now, or during the Great War, or the Holocaust… Perhaps an instant's shuteye for God is an eon for us… Bound to miss things, especially if you're tired… Maybe God was tired; of me; of the Creation; of everything…* Well, that was okay. He was not angry at God. Frustrated, but not angry: he understood God's position.

Falling… like a giant leaf on this beautiful, late summer morning…

Faces took on resemblances now. Some old lady was screaming, pointing up at him. All the people around her were watching him fall, but she was the only one screaming.

He didn't have all the time in the world after all: He'd been mistaken about that.

The comforting pavement met Roger Anderson… and all was as it should be.

This is the kind of party you never want to attend—as my hard-drinking protagonist, David Ashland, is about to find out…

—WFN

ASHLAND

The long dark limo motors smoothly through the fog-thick night. A uniformed chauffeur, Sidney, is at the wheel. A glass partition separates him from David and Lydia Ashland, the tight-faced couple in the car's back seat. David Ashland is puffy, with swollen eyes. Alcohol has flushed his usually pale skin.

Lydia glares at her husband. Her features are hawkish. "Congratulations. You made a total fool of yourself."

David Ashland closes his eyes, leaning back into pliant leather. "I was being funny. I'm always funny at parties."

"Do you consider it funny to pour a whiskey sour over the hostess?"

"Accident. I was trying to climb up on the piano. To sing. Very funny song."

"You got us thrown out of the party."

"No sense of humor, those jerks. I was funny."

"You were disgusting. Vulgar and disgusting."

He leans forward, eyes bright with anger. "I'll tell you what was vulgar and disgusting—the way you went after that guitar player."

She snorts. "I have to find affection *somewhere*. God knows you don't supply it ... "

He closes his eyes again, his back against the seat. "You get back what you give out in this world, sweetie. And you're one helluva cold fish."

Strained silence as the limo purrs through the darkness.

Lydia continues to glare at her husband. "This kind of life... it killed your first wife."

"Trish drank herself to death. I can handle booze. She couldn't."

"You pushed her over the edge. She drank just to keep from going crazy. Same as I do. For the same reasons."

Ashland shifts in the seat to face her. "Don't give me that shit! You drink because you *like* it. Nobody puts a gun to your head."

Another tense silence. Then: "David, I'm divorcing you."

He shrugs, easing back. "Fine. Do it. I don't need you in my life."

"No, all you need is another party, another vodka martini, another crowd to play the fool for."

His reply is edged. "Just shut up about what I need."

Sidney swings the limo onto the freeway, into a cloudy swirl of heavy ground fog. The sudden harsh sound of a truck's airhorn stabs the night. A semi is headed straight at them.

Ashland slams a fist against the glass, shouting, "Sidney, look out!"

The chauffeur twists the wheel violently and the big limo slides sideways across the fog-slick asphalt. They are enveloped in a wall of fog.

Whiteout.

A shift in reality. A ripple in Time...

Sidney rolls back the glass pane. "Sorry, Mr. Ashland. My fault entirely."

Ashland nods as Sidney leaves the freeway. Soon the limo glides through a plush neighborhood lined with stately mansions. The car rolls smoothly up a pebbled drive to the Ashland home. Tall. Imposing.

Sidney opens the rear passenger door and David Ashland steps out. Lydia remains inside. "Aren't you coming?" he snaps.

"No, I'm *going.* Away from you. To my sister's. I don't want to go into that house with you tonight."

"Suit yourself. What about the car?"

"Sidney will bring it back after dropping me off."

"Fine. I'm going in and having a drink."

Her tone is mocking. "Now where have I heard *that* before?"

The limo drifts off into darkness as Ashland enters the house.

He tosses aside his topcoat, walks into the den, moves to the wall bar, and pours himself a Scotch. Drink in hand, he settles into a chair by the fireplace , muttering aloud: "So go run off to your sis. Great. Ole Davy here will make out just fine without you."

He dozes—to be jolted awake by the front door chime. The chauffeur is back.

"What is it, Sidney?" He peers over Sidney's left shoulder at the parked limo outside. "Why isn't the car in the garage?"

"I assumed you would wish to use it, sir."

"Use it! It's after three in the morning!"

Sidney nods calmly. "Mrs. Ashland wants you to join her at a party."

"I thought she was going to . . . " He breaks off. "Is she serious? About a party?"

"Very much so. She asked me to drive you there."

David grins. "Well, I've never turned one down yet."

The road is deserted as the limo motors smoothly through the night. The city is quiet, a vast tomb of silence.

"So where's this party? At the Milton's? I hear the Sterns are back from Europe. Is it their party?"

"No, sir. The party is downtown."

"But I don't know anybody downtown."

"It's a new apartment building, sir."

Ashland relaxes against the seat. "Okay, okay, I'm game. Drive on, McDuff!"

The limo pulls up in front of a modern steel-and-glass building. The structure glows with light from a dozen windows.

David gets out. "What floor?"

"The penthouse, sir." Sidney smiles. "Have a good time, Mr. Ashland."

David smiles back. "I always do … "

The lobby smells of fresh paint and polished brass. A plush blue carpet muffles his steps as he rings for the elevator. He is alone in the vast lobby. No doorman or guard.

The elevator doors slide back and he enters the enclosure, thumbing the "P" button.

He arrives at the penthouse, knocks briskly. Party sounds filter out to him: a sea tide of voices, the tinkle of iced drinks, the thump of festive music.

A fat, sweaty man opens the door. "Hey, dude! Come join the party!"

Ashland steps inside, into an expansive living room crowded with a mass of guests. The room is decorated in an Asian motif: Jade tables with serpent legs, lavishly painted screens, standing lamps with jewel-eyed dragons looped at their base, and at the room's far end an immense bronze gong, suspended between a pair of demon-faced warriors.

A thin, sharp-faced woman with a turkey neck and heavily blackened lashes taps David on the shoulder. "You look like a man I saw once outside the town library when I was a child. He was sitting quietly on a wooden bench … " She giggles.

"He had his throat cut ear to ear."

Ashland walks quickly away from her, threading through the crowd to a bar at the far side of the room.

As he pours himself a drink, as a dyed blonde sidles up to him. "Hi, I'm Vivian. I drink a lot."

Ashland is at a loss to reply. He mutters, "That's nice."

"No, it's lousy! I keep drinking but I can't get smashed. Are you smashed?"

David ignores her question. "I'm looking for my wife. Her name is Lydia. Tall, with short hair, wearing a—"

The woman looks angry. "I never help bastards find their wives!"

She wheels off into the crowd.

A fever-eyed man approaches him. "If you wish to maintain your health you can't just *stand* there! Keep moving. Stay ahead of them."

"Them?"

"Germs. They form clouds around people. Unless you keep moving, they'll gang up on you. Billions of 'em. It's terrible!"

"I'll keep that in mind," David replies.

The man starts away. "Better get trotting!"

A tap on his left arm. David turns to face a stooped, cadaver-thin man in black, with a plump snake curled around his neck. "Her name is Baby and she likes to rest her head against your neck. Not afraid of snakes, are you?"

"Can't say I'm fond of them."

The bony man nods: "Want to hold her?"

"Uh… *no*. No thanks." And he moves away.

David scans the smoke-hazed room and sees a figure he believes may be Lydia heading into the kitchen. David shouts her name, but she's gone.

Ashland quickly enters the kitchen, stopping to question

a bearded man. "My wife... tall, green dress. She just came in here. Did you see her?"

The bearded man sighs. His eyes reflect sadness. "I no longer look at women. Can't do anything with them, so why look at them?"

"I came in here looking for my wife."

The shaggy man grunts. "And *I'm* looking for a way out of this party!"

Ashland edges away from him, bumping into a dark, elf-like woman. She holds up an unlit cigar. "Light?"

David fumbles for his cigarette lighter, thumbs it to flame, igniting her cigar. She inhales, blowing smoke from her nose. "Been smoking cigs till tonight. Thought I'd try a cigar, but it's got no kick." She regards him with an intense stare. "You seem alone. Are you?"

He shakes his head. "My wife's here somewhere."

"I haven't been alone since Milwaukee," she says. "I was maybe fourteen and this creep moves in with me. Is your wife a creep?"

"Most of the time. She wants to divorce me. Says I drink too much."

"Do you?"

"Of course not!"

"So... this creep moves in and things are bad from the git-go. That's why I killed him."

"You—you *what?*"

"Shot the sucker. Three times in the head!" She points a finger at Ashland. "Bang! Bang! Bang!"

Ashland frowns. "I—I have to find my wife."

A man with a mop of fire truck red hair grips David's arm. "I lost me a wife once. Greek belly dancer with a Jersey accent... She used to quote that line of Hemingway's to Scott Fitzgerald. One that goes 'We're all bitched from the start.'

Bitter, bitter line, huh?"

"Yes, it's—"

"I'm Terry Travers. Good name for an actor. My real one's shitty. Remember the old *Triple Trouble for Terry* series on TV?"

"Can't say that I—"

"Had to step on a few folks to get that show." He snaps open his wallet to display a photo. "This is me before I did the show. Total baldie! Mr. Chromedome."

"Uh … yes, I see."

"I wear rugs now. Top quality. Handsewn." Inclines his head. "Go ahead—tug at it!"

"I'll take your word," Ashland replies.

"Aw, c'mon. As a personal favor to me. Give it a tug."

Ashland complies without enthusiasm.

"Snug, eh? Really sticks to the old noggin. Got a windblown one for outdoor stuff. Got a crew-cut for Army flicks. Got me one with sideburns for oaters … "

"Good for you."

"Know where the word 'sideburns' comes from?"

"Can't say as I do." David looks around for Lydia, anxious to leave the bald man.

"Guy named Burnside. Dumbass Civil War general. Wore his hair down each side of his face. So 'sideburns' got named after him, only backwards. Burnside … sideburns. Get it?"

"I do. I get it."

"I don't act anymore. I just booze. Me and six million alcoholics."

"My wife's here somewhere. I need to find her."

"It's all about illusion," says Travers. "Reality versus illusion. A lie often reveals truth, but the truth is often a lie."

Ashland has had enough. He exits the kitchen.

Someone calls out to him. "Hey, you! You leaving the kitchen!"

A flush-faced man in a sateen dinner jacket waves to David from the center of the room. He is standing on a chair. "A moment of your time, sir."

Ashland approaches him. "You talking to me?"

"Might I borrow that ring you're wearing?"

"Well, I really don't—"

"No harm will come to it, I assure you." He reaches out a hand. "If you please, sir."

Reluctantly Ashland slips off his gold wedding ring, handing it to the man in the chair.

He presses the ring to his forehead. "Ahhh... let me read the vibrations." A dramatic pause. "Your first name begins with a 'D'... Not Daniel... or Dexter... Ah, *David*... Am I correct?"

"Yes. Yes, I'm David Ashland."

"You are talented... an *architect*... and rich." Another pause. "But you have not worked for your money. It is your *father's* money."

Ashland's face is tight; he does not find this amusing.

"You like women... have married two of them. Have never been faithful... And you like to drink. Too much. Far too much."

Ashland thrusts out a hand. "That's enough, damn you! My ring!"

The smiling man hands back the ring. David stalks to the bar and pours a fresh whiskey. He settles into a couch by the window, drink in hand, his face red and sweating. A dough-faced man with a pencil-thin mustache sits down on the couch beside him.

He leans close. "Do you worry a lot? My mother worries about the Earth slowing down. She read somewhere that between 1680 and 1690 the Earth lost two one-hundredths of a second in its orbit around the Sun. She said that was a bad sign."

Ashland stands. "I don't mean to be rude but I can't talk right now."

The man nods. “So don’t! I’ll do the talking. Talking is my business: I’m a salesman. Dover Insurance. Like the White Cliffs of, ya know. You meet a lot of fruitcakes in my game. Sold a policy once to a guy who lived in the woodwork. Spent all his time inside this foldaway bed in the wall. Had a real sour temper. Didn’t care for most people … ” He draws in a breath, then continues the flow of words. “One night his roommate invited some friends over and their noise woke up the fruitcake guy. Out he pops from his bed in the wall with a loaded Thompson sub-machine gun in his hands, yelling for them all to get the hell out of his apartment. He was ready to cut loose with the Thompson!”

“That’s crazy!”

A voice behind Ashland: “I knew a fella who was *twice* that crazy … ”

David shifts uncomfortably, facing a man hairy as a gorilla with rheumy eyes lost behind bottle-thick glasses. “He lived up in Vermont,” the hairy man relates, “and he believed in falling grandmothers.”

“I don’t … ” began David.

“*Watch out for falling grandmothers*, he’d say. *They come down pretty heavy during the early winter … Carry umbrellas and big packages and they come floating down out of the sky by the thousands!* This Vermont guy *swore* he saw a postal worker killed by one. Awful thing to witness he told me. Knocked him flat. Crushed his head like an eggshell … ”

The Dover Insurance salesman cuts in: “Gosh, I knew a guy who called himself a creative writer. Claimed he couldn’t write on paper: Too flimsy. So he’d rent a house and scrawl these novels of his on the walls and ceilings with a big black crayon. Chapter in every room. When he finished a novel he’d rent another house for the next one.”

The gorilla man asks: “Was he any good?”

"Dunno. I never read any of his houses."

Ashland stands up. His glass is empty. "I need to get another drink."

"Waste of time," says the salesman. "Won't get you blotto. Booze is no good here... no damn good at all."

Ashland moves to the bar where a frost-haired blonde in sequins sways close to him. "I have a theory about sleep. Care to hear it?"

Ashland is sweaty, nervous, on edge. "Not really."

"My theory is that we all go insane each night when our subconscious takes control. We become helpless victims to whatever it conjures up. Our conscious mind is totally out of it. We lie there, powerless, while our subconscious pushes us off cliffs and tall buildings, throws us in front of speeding trains, buries us alive... We have absolutely no control as the mind whirls madly in our skull." She peers intently at him. "Isn't that unsettling to think about?"

"Very. Now, if you'll excuse me—"

She grips his arm tightly. "I wrote a poem about it. Care to hear it?"

"I'm not much for poetry."

Her voice rises: "In the skulled winding sheet/Of the blooded nightmare/we sand-crawl/ The hallways of madness."

To David, the party sounds seem louder, more strident.

The blonde leans very close to him, her breath rank. "Sometimes, even when you're awake, your mind can play awful tricks on you. Like one morning, I woke up in bed to find this big *spider-thing* on my pillow. It was *huge!* Like the size of a *baby*. Right there in bed with me! Well, you can imagine what I—"

Ashland pushes away from her. "Sorry, but I need to find my wife."

In the crowd a hand touches his shoulder. "Sidney! What are *you* doing here?"

The chauffeur has his jacket off, and his shirt is unbuttoned. "I was invited," he says. "We were *all* invited."

"I—I don't understand."

"Been looking for Mrs. Ashland?"

"Yes, I—"

"She's around. You'll see her."

Sidney fades into the heated crowd.

"Wait!"

Ashland starts after him, but is engulfed in the tide of partygoers. Voices assail him from all sides.

"So he took the Luger and *blew her head off*..."

"The X-rays *destroyed* his white cells..."

"Found her in the tub: strangled with a *coat hanger*..."

"He had a *Grade Two* epidermal carcinoma at the base of a seborrhea keratosis..."

"Potatoes have eyes: I really *believe* that..."

"*Big* tiger moth. No bones inside. Just dusted away when I smashed him against the glass..."

"Found her tied up in a laundry bag in his car trunk. *Her legs were missing*..."

"Unfortunately, med schools won't accept a *corpse* more than twelve hours old..."

"When a man is shot in the brain his *eyes* go black..."

"*Never* sign your name in blood..."

In a staggered panic, Ashland smashes his way through the partygoers toward the Asian gong on the far wall. "Got to stop... all this!" He drives his right fist hard against the bronze gong. It trembles under the blow, *but there is no sound.* The stifling tide of party chatter continues; no one seems to have noticed David's frantic action.

A dark-haired, overly made-up woman leans close to him. "No use, darlin'. You can't stop the *party!*"

David gasps: "I—I'm leaving!"

"So go," she says, smiling. "Nobody cares."

He rushes out to the hallway elevator, jamming a thumb against the Lobby button. The doors open … to Lydia. "Been looking for me, Davy?"

Ashland is pale, badly shaken. "What—what's going on? That party … it's *insane.*"

She grins. "But I thought you *loved* parties."

"Not this one. This one is … horrible!"

The elevator suddenly stops at Floor 2, and Trish, David's first wife, steps inside. "Hi, sweetie: long time no see!"

Ashland is in shock. "But … But you're—"

"Dead?" she asks. "Yeah, we *all* are … "

"Oh! She's right … " Lydia chuckles.

He stares numbly at them. "The … The truck … on … on the freeway … "

"It *hit* us, David," says Lydia. "You … me … Sidney … we didn't *survive.*"

The lobby doors click open and Ashland runs toward the street exit, but the outer door is securely locked. David pounds on the glass.

Inside the elevator, the two women giggle. "No use, lover. You can't leave the party: it's just getting started!"

Ashland swings around, wild-eyed and panting. He runs down the long hallway, passing a series of apartments: 1D … 1E … 1F …

Exhausted, he falls against one of the doors at the end of the hall, begins pounding on it. "Help! Somebody help me!"

A fat, sweaty man opens the door. "Hey, dude! Come join the party!"

David screams.

This is based on a personal fantasy—being able to go back in the past and pick up several copies of the first appearance of Superman, which is now worth a fortune…
Here, the fantasy is realized.

—WFN

MILLIKIN'S MACHINE

If you're reading these words, then you've found the bottle with this account inside that I tossed into the Missouri River. I needed to set the record straight on what happened to me and Herold.

I've known Herold Millikin for a large part of my life. We both graduated from Oak Forest High together. Not much of a school in not much of a town in rural Missouri, about eighty miles east of Kansas City. Small class. Only about three dozen other seniors graduated with us. I knew most of them, but Herold was my best friend. We did everything together: played on the school basketball team, attended cowboy movies at the old Gillham theater, went roller skating with the Abernathey girls (Herold got to date the cute one while I was stuck with her mud-ugly sister who looked like a bulldog in heat). We played weekend pool at Eddie's bar, putting away a lot of ginger ale. (Herold trimmed me four games out of five.)

One thing we didn't share. Herold was absolutely fruitcake for Golden Age superhero comics. Except for *Superman*, he had complete runs of his favorite titles: *Batman, Green Lantern, The Flash, Human Torch, Captain America, Hawkman, Sub-Mariner*, and a slew of others. I didn't share his passion. To me, comic books were dumb. But Herold was a fanatic. Comics were his Holy Grail.

Then World War II came along and Herold's mother donated his entire collection to the scrap drive while Herold was visiting a friend in St. Louis. Back home, he went bonkers. Yelled and screamed like a demented monkey, then brooded darkly about his loss for months. Like the bottom had fallen out of his life.

I went on to open a small deli in Evanston and lost track of Herold. He stayed in Oak Forest, got married and divorced the same year, and worked in the town paper mill with his Dad. Aside from a card at Christmas, we were not in touch. Then, one day out of the blue, I get this really weird phone call from him.

"I'm in trouble," he said. "I need your help, Sam." (That's my name—Sam Burns.)

"Hey, man, what's the trouble?"

"It's gonna sound super crazy to you."

"I can handle crazy, so go ahead. By the way, where are you? You calling from Oak Forest? Got a lot of static—"

"I'm calling from 33rd and Troost in K.C. Outside Ray's Drug Store."

"On a pay phone?"

"Not exactly. It's a … *chrono-phone.*"

"A *what*?"

"It's the only thing that still works on my machine! I set it up so I could phone back to where you are in 2012. I'm in 1938 now." There was a pause, then he added: "I'm calling you on a type of *time* phone. That's what a chrono-phone is."

"This is really crazy," I said. I laughed, but nothing was funny.

"Well, I warned you," declared Herold. "Listen … will

you just bear with me? For old times' sake. There's nobody else I can turn to."

"Turn to for what?"

His tone was desperate. "Lemme explain. While I was in the drug store a bunch of nasty schoolkids used my machine for a crapper and pissed all over the inside. Shorted out all the wiring. Left me stuck here. The chrono-phone is the only part that still works."

I drew in a deep breath. "Okay, let's start over. Just where the hell are you calling from?"

"I *told* you—from 33rd and Troost in Kansas City."

"What are you doing there?"

"Ray carries all the latest comics. Knew he'd have what I wanted. And I got it!"

"Got what?"

"The first issue of *Action Comics.* June, 1938. Just printed. Mint copy. With the debut of Superman. It's cherry!"

"Okay, Herold, I'll play the game. You say you're in 1938?"

"Right."

"So how did you *get* to 1938?"

"In my time machine. It worked fine till those brats pissed in it."

"Have you been drinking? Taking drugs? Are you stoned?"

"No, no … I'm perfectly fine. It's just that I need to get back to 2012—which is why I'm calling you."

"Let me get this straight. You are calling me on a freaking *time* phone from 1938?"

"Yeah, yeah, now you're getting it! I came here to buy the comic book. Thing's worth a fortune! One issue sold for over two million at auction. Once I get back and sell my mint issue of *Action Comics* I'll be a rich man."

I decided to play along with Herold. Something had obviously snapped in his brain, but before I could arrange for him to get medical attention, I needed to hear him out. "Just what do you want from me, Herold?"

"I need you to build *another* time machine and come here to 1938. Then we'll both use it to get back to 2012."

"And just how am I supposed to build a time machine?"

"You go to my garage in Oak Forest. You've been there plenty of times, watching me build stuff. The plans I worked out for the time machine are all there in a blue notebook on the back shelf. Just follow my notes."

"I'm no big hand with machinery," I told him. "Hell, I can barely change a light bulb!"

"It's a piece of cake! Like I said, just follow my notes. It's all there. You can do it, Sam. I'm depending on you."

"This is insane."

"No, it's perfectly logical: You build the new machine and come back in it to 1938 where I'll be waiting inside Ray's drug store. Then we use it to hop back to 2012. Piece of cake."

It wasn't. A piece of cake, that is. I decided to call his bluff and drove back to Oak Forest. His dad let me into the garage—where I found the blue notebook. They were all there. The complete plans for Millikin's machine. It took me a full week, with Herold's dad wondering what the devil I was up to in his son's garage, but I did it. I built a brand-new time machine.

Another call. "Is it done? Did you build it?"

"Yep, by God I did."

"I've been sleeping on a hardwood floor in the storage room here at Ray's. It's murder on my back and my butt's killing me. When can you get here?"

"If the dingus works the way you say it does I'll be there early tomorrow."

"Sam, you're a peach. I'll be waiting."

And the next morning I stepped inside the contraption and took off for 1938.

There he was. My old pal, Herold, standing in front of Ray's at 33rd and Troost, grinning like a fool and clutching his mint copy of *Action Comics.* He hadn't changed much in the years since I'd seen him last, still jug-eared and big-nosed, with lots of wrinkles. Only major difference: he'd lost most of his hair since high school. His pate was bald as a bat.

"You made it!" he said to me as I stepped out of his infernal machine.

"Yep, I made it." I looked around. "So this is 1938."

"I had faith in you, Sam. Knew you could do it!"

We embraced, with me being careful not to crush his copy of *Action Comics.* He turned the pages gently, the way you'd handle the Dead Sea Scrolls, showing me Superman as poorly drawn by Joe Shuster. A lousy artist, he could never quite get the "S" right on Superman's chest, but I had to admit that he and Jerry Siegel had created an icon, the first of the great comic book superheroes.

"What now? " I asked.

"Now we head back to 2012," he said, looking cow-like and contented, easing the comic book into a leather case. "It's fireproof," he told me.

"Dandy," I said.

We stepped into the time machine: It was a bit crowded for two. Herold surveyed the interior—a maze of dials and buttons and blinking lights. He wrinkled his nose and then cleared his throat. "Crude," he said. He noticed I was glaring at him, then added: "But obviously effective!" He pressed a green button and the wall screen came alive, filled with spinning numbers.

"Gotta set it *just* right," Herold told me. He fiddled with an orange knob, and a date swam into view on the screen:

DESTINATION 2012

"Okey-doke," said Herold, throwing a shiny switch below the screen. "We're on the way!"

With a loud humming and a dizzy swirl of colors, we were off for 2012.

We never got there.

When the machine stopped a new message flashed across the glowing time screen:

WELCOME TO 1928

Ray's drug store was a shoe repair shop. A trolley car rumbled past on Troost with a big red sign on its side:

SMOKE HEALTHY!
NINE OUT OF TEN DOCTORS PREFER
CHESTERFIELDS

Herold snatched a newspaper from a metal rack in front of the shoe store. The headline read: MOVIE MOGUL SAYS TALKIES ARE A FAD

And under that: AGENTS RAID 20 SPEAKEASIES

A Skelly station across the street posted gas for twenty-one cents a gallon.

"This is vexing," declared Herold. "We went *backward* instead of forward."

I stared at him. "What went wrong?"

Herold squinted at a section of blackened tubes. "Looks like the Epoch Calculator has fused to the Geosynchrous Stabilizer. With proper tools I can fix it."

"Then *do* it! We can't stay stuck here in 1928!"

He hesitated, sucking at his lower lip. "There's another problem."

"Which is?"

"All my tools are in the garage." He sighed. "Back in Oak Forest."

"That's a fine kettle of fish," I said.

Luckily, we were able to find a tool store on 32nd where Herold was able to buy what he needed. But it took all the cash we had.

While he worked on the machine I ambled here and there, absorbing 1928. A new car cost just five hundred dollars and you could buy a two-story house for seven thousand. A loaf of bread cost nine cents and there were ads in the paper for something called "Psychic Base Ball." Walt Disney released a black-and-white cartoon called *Steamboat Willie.* Every newsstand carried a wide variety of gaudy pulp magazines, and White Castle hamburgers were six for a quarter. You could get a full meal with coffee and dessert for just thirty-five cents, including the tip.

Only one day after our arrival, Herold announced: "Got it fixed! We should be able to get back to 2012 with no sweat."

"Great!" I pumped his hand. "Herold, you're a genius."

"Yeah," he admitted sheepishly. "I guess I am."

And off we went, headed for 2012.

That was when we survived the mishap. Obviously.

Dials and cogwheels and computer chips rained down around us as Millikin's machine imploded, blowing itself into rainbow fragments. And, this time, Herold couldn't use the chrono-phone; it was a lump of smoking, heat-fused metal.

When the smoke cleared a message sputtered to life on the cracked screen:

WELCOME TO 2213

I turned to Herold with a scowl. I could feel that my face was red and my eyes were stinging: "*Now* what do you say?"

He blinked soot-blackened eyes at me, shrugging. "I must have reversed the wiring."

"So what do we do now?"

"We do the only thing we *can* do," he replied. "We live out the rest of our lives in 2213."

"And just what do we live *on*? You spent the last of our cash in that tool store."

He held up the fireproof leather case containing *Action Comics.* "Piece of cake. We sell this for say half a million—a real bargain price—and bam! Our financial worries are over!"

All the buildings in the future are tall and glittery and there are plenty of family rockets. We located a spaceship-shaped store called Truly Fat Frank's with a metallic sign in the window: We buy *anything* for top dollar! We walked inside.

"Hello there," said Herold to the corpulent man behind the counter. "You must be Truly Fat Frank."

"That's me," the decidedly overweight man said, nodding toward the leather case that Herold placed gently on the counter top. "Whatcha got there?"

"A rare treasure indeed," said Herold, his voice swelling with pride. "Inside this case is the first issue of *Action Comics,* featuring the birth of Superman! A legendary comic book."

Truly Fat Frank rubbed a pudgy hand along his jaw. He stared at Herold. "What's a comic book? Is it funny?"

Herold gulped audibly. "You mean you've never—"

"Is it digital, or carbonfibre?"

"Uh, no, it's . . . *paper.*"

Frank shook his bloated head. "*Paper?* Nobody reads paper stuff anymore. Went out of fashion when they cut the last tree down back in 2100. Paper stuff is worthless, and not politically correct. Everything is digital or carbonfibre. You boys ain't local, are you? You from Alpha Centauri or something?"

He opened the leather case, squinting at the comic book. "Tellya what . . . I like your faces so much, against my better judgment, I'm gonna buy this . . . *paper* thing."

"That's very kind of you," said Herold.

The store owner pursed his lips. "So how's about five million credits?"

Herold stared at Frank, his eyes wide. He nodded.

The proprietor smiled and reached under the counter. "Oh—how do you want that? E-currency or physical credits? I collect old paper money, too—"

Herold licked his lips, head thrusting forward in astonishment. "Paper money, please." His voice cracked slightly before he regained his composure. "Paper, please, *not* plastic." He winked at Frank.

The owner shrugged and produced the bills.

Herold gestured with a trembling hand as the owner counted out ten dollars.

That was when Herold started to cry.

So, if you're still reading this, we have a favor to ask.

Go to the garage at 1537 North Pitts Street in Oak Forest, Missouri, where you'll find a blue notebook full of instructions. Tell Herold's father that he sent you to work in the garage, but don't show him this account. The old geezer has a bad heart and might pop off. Follow the instructions in the blue notebook and build a new time machine. All the spare parts are there.

We are in an alley in the year 2213, just off 31st and Troost in Kansas City. Our clothes are in rags and we drink wine out of a nanocarbon sack.

Please rescue us. We smell bad.

Real bad.

For a long while now, I've been curious about what would happen if something like the following story came to pass: How would my characters react? How would I? This story provides my thoughts about this difficult subject.

—WFN

THE END: A FINAL DIALOGUE

(for Jason and Sunni Brock)

HIM: I've often wondered how we'd die. Now I know.

HER: Funny ... I don't feel like crying. I thought I would, but I'm not going to. I just feel *numb* ...

HIM: Wouldn't change anything anyway. We can only accept reality. It's happening, and nothing can stop it. They've tried everything. Nothing's worked.

HER: You'd think that with all this technology that we could stop it somehow. At least slow it down.

HIM: Well, they tried. They waited to see if it would change on its own ... They attempted subtle manipulation ... They called in specialists from all over the world ... They even tried brute force, evasive actions; it's nobody's fault, just the way these things happen sometimes.

HER: Why can't they irradiate it?

HIM: They looked into that and concluded that would only make it spread. Instead of *one* we'd have a slew of them. The net result would be the same, maybe even worse.

HER: Perhaps it'll burn out—

HIM: It's too large to burn out ...

HER: Maybe if we'd moved away from here we could have avoided all of this.

HIM: It wouldn't matter where we lived, you know that. There's no escaping fate.

HER: Where did it come from?

HIM: Who knows? A rogue element... Something just a little off. Doesn't take much to disrupt everything, does it?

HER: I had a really vivid dream last night. About our honeymoon—when we went to the Outer Banks of North Carolina...

HIM: That was such a wonderful time.

HER: Remember the beautiful sea turtle we found with the cut on her flipper?

HIM: Of course! You insisted on fixing her up, so we wrapped her leg in a bandage. Called her Cinnamon, after the Neil Young song. Bandage probably only lasted a few minutes once she was back in the water! I felt good about it, though, and was so glad we assisted her.

HER: Me, too. It was so caring the way you spread the salve on her. When she looked up at us with her big, brown, shiny eyes... I know she was thanking us.

HIM: Then we helped her get back into the water. I could swear she looked back one last time before she disappeared into the Atlantic.

HER: You took so many pictures of Cinnamon! We still have them in our album.

HIM: I took a lot of picture on that trip!

HER: It was a perfect honeymoon... and, now, none of it seems to matter.

HIM: No. It matters. It *always* matters. We matter to each other, to Cinnamon. We've made a difference. Could it have been longer? Could it have been less rough along the way? Sure, but scars are a record... They mean we were *here*, that we tried things, and weren't just exiles in some dark remote place, avoiding life... existing, but not really *living*. It means we weren't afraid to be hurt, and that's everything in the long run. It's *all* there is, really.

HER: The specialists seemed so confident at first. How much time do we have?

HIM: Not much. But then, how much do any of us ever really have? At present, not even another hour, probably.

HER: Still, it all seems so pointless now... We had such potential. How fast the years have gone! I was almost done with my certificate... And you were about to be promoted again...

HIM: I know. It's a long way from where we started, huh? You had the best profile on the 'net, and the hottest picture! But it's not pointless. Death finds us all in good time, and in whatever way is deemed appropriate, and it doesn't matter what our plans are, great or small. Once it's time, it's time—whether from dementia, cancer, or a killer asteroid that wipes all life from the Earth at once. It's up to us to maximize the span between comprehension of the terminal moment and our final end, whatever it may be.

HER: I know you're right. All I wanted was an intelligent, strong man in my life... with a good sense of humor. The opposite of my father. Remember the first time we talked on the phone? Three hours straight! I realized you were the one right from the start.

HIM: You didn't act like it. You seemed cautious... reserved.

HER: I was playing close to the vest. When I saw your picture... when we talked... you seemed too good to be true. I've never looked at another man since.

HIM: Well, I'd looked at a lot of other women before, but none measured up to you.

HER: And now we've come to the end.

HIM: It's like the old cliché: Every road has an ending.

HER: We've had a good life together.

HIM: The best.

HER: Any regrets?

HIM: A few, but none that bear repeating. Do you think we'll see each other again? Afterward?

HER: Yes, I do. I know we'll be together ... and the babies, too. Will there be pain ... when it happens, I mean? I'm not good with pain.

HIM: When it happens we'll die instantly. There should be no pain.

HER: You've made me so happy!

HIM: That's all I've ever wanted to do ... to make you happy.

HER: You've been a wonderful husband.

HIM: And you've been a wonderful wife. I love you.

HER: I love you, too! So much ... Look! The sky ... all turned to fire!

HIM: It ... It's time—

HER: Hold me!

Blackness.

This story began as an exercise in writing about an area of one of Mr. Nolan's personal interests: World War II. I challenged him to create a story about it, as we both felt the horrors of war were as frightening as any supernatural entity or monster could be. After Bill's first draft, we re-wrote the story completely, making it grittier, more character-driven, more terrifying… In addition, we made the decisions to separate the action from a specific place and time, and mix up the linearity of the plot—this could be any war, at any time, on any planet, and friend or foe is completely in the eye of the beholder…

—JVB

THE BEACH

(with Jason V Brock)

"Left 'em back on the beach, Emilie . . . ," Ivan said. "Back on the beach with Lars."

The chaos of death surrounded him . . . shrouded him . . . numbed him . . .

In the rosy chill of dawn and drifting smoke, Ivan saw:

A leg severed at the hip by machine-gun fire . . .

A flower of spilled guts from an artillery shell . . .

Blood everywhere, staining the sand, crimsoning the water . . .

Sprawled bodies suddenly devoid of life . . . Shocked faces . . . Wildly staring eyes . . . Curses . . . Prayers . . . Pieces of comrades, parts of strangers: all belonging to members of their group . . .

"This is it!" Lars screamed, frightened eyes wide; those were his last words before he ate a mortar shell, reducing his head to a helmet full of red jelly.

Nothing else in the world stopped, nothing else changed as his broken frame slumped to the hard ground . . .

Whispering voices rumbled through the cold air as the regiment stood in formation, waiting. Ivan felt nervous; his hands were damp, his mouth dry.

After nearly an hour, a large door at the opposite end of their dimly lit confines scraped open, and a small phalanx of people walked in from another room. They stood in a rigid cluster at the front of the long line of men, silhouetted by the intense glare of field lamps; they, too, appeared to be waiting.

Abruptly, a short, bespectacled colonel snapped his boot heels together and held up a silencing hand, moving purposefully to the front of the group. The room quieted, and the tension in the chamber mounted; finally, there was the sound of heavy boots moving in a slow procession.

Then Ivan caught his first glimpse of the General: In the periphery of his vision, he could sense the man's presence, and a smile spread over his face. This is it . . .

The old warrior seemed surprisingly informal—even relaxed—as he socialized with the men, confiding to the soldiers as he made his way past them, flanked by his junior officers. After a long while, it was Ivan's turn: his head was pounding in anticipation.

"You look young! How old are you, son?" the General asked, shaking Ivan's hand; his skin was soft, warm. Ivan detected the faintest hint of Bourbon in the air.

"Twenty-one, sir."

The senior officer chuckled, the lines of his face creasing in amusement: "An old man, eh?"

"Old man? Why-why I suppose so, sir!" Ivan felt himself blush, but held the General's gaze as the man wished him luck; the assemblage moved further down the way. The sadness in the man's eyes was telling: Ivan suspected that the General knew he was already conferring with a legion of ghosts.

Distantly, Ivan heard him chatting with his best friend Lars, a lanky kid near the end of the line: "Are you scared, son?"

"Scared? N-No, sir!" Lars exclaimed. There was a moment of quiet.

"Well," the General said at last, his voice weary, soft. "I am . . . "

Now the fighting began in earnest: Enemy planes pirouetted above, gleaming in the sun, which had burned off the morning haze . . . Shots careened and ricocheted in invisible fury . . . Heavy artillery rocked the ground, their shattering explosions punishing the air . . .

One of the shells finally landed too close to Ivan: Pulling a shaky hand away from his ear, he saw that it was covered in blood. When he looked up, he realized that everything was suddenly muffled, as if his head was packed with wet cotton. His eardrums had been ruptured in the blast.

Before he could decide a course of action, Ivan felt a solid shove at his back, and reflexively turned to see what it was, catching a glimpse of Lars' limp, dirt covered body and demolished head. The boy was still sitting next to him, clutching his rifle as though waiting to fire it.

"I said: *UP, Soldier!*" The order from his commanding officer brought Ivan back to reality; he could only tell what the man was yelling by watching his lips. "There's nothing more you can do here!" Explosions and flak were everywhere, strafing the ground, but Ivan's suddenly quieted world removed him from the mind-searing horror of the moment. Rifle in hand, he turned his attention back to the battle, to survival. *Maybe I'll be next. Lars didn't make it . . . Maybe I won't either . . .*

In front of him, a Viennese waltz of mayhem played out in his terribly silenced world: Men twirled in horrifying slow motion, completely engulfed by flames on the reddening sandscape . . . Airplanes spiraled into the sea, plumes of black smoke trailing like a comet's tail before exploding on the water's white-capped surface . . . Even the water itself was darkening—stained as red as burgundy with blood... Great geysers of sand, bone, and flesh randomly spewed into the sky from detonating mines... Some men just fell over, looking for all the world like toys in a child's game, or dreamy recollections of an old movie...

And Ivan heard none of it.

His father—a coldly rational doctor not prone to praise or affection—rarely spoke to him. His mother—Catholic, repressed—did little to smooth their interaction. As an only child, Ivan had felt closest to her growing up. Her death from cancer when he was seventeen had been devastating. His father died a few years later, literally and figuratively of a broken heart.

Shortly after his mother passed away, Ivan met Emilie. Even though he was a year older than she was, her parents allowed them to get engaged just before he left for college. Ivan was gone for nearly a year as a pre-med student at the University, working away the loneliness of many empty nights at a local drug store—his only way to pay for school. He visited home—a week's train ride away—when he had the time and extra money.

Once the war began, Ivan enlisted—against his father's objections—because he felt it was the right thing to do. School would have to wait: duty and honor came first.

Ivan and Emilie married just ahead of his admission into the military, and though they'd never spent that much time together, Ivan loved her deeply. All that mattered was that he knew she loved him, too.

Now, coming up on his eighth month in battle, he yearned to be home. Just before leaving once more for the Front, he posted what could be, for all he knew, his final letter to her:

> Dearest Emilie,
>
> It looks like we'll be making a big assault in the very near future. It won't be like the

others: it's another animal, so to speak. I can't say when or where, please understand.

Things are heating up fast, rumors are flying. We've been put on special alert; everyone is excited and scared, including me.

We'd be fools not to be afraid of what's waiting for us… We know we'll be heading into a firestorm; the position is heavily armored, due to its strategic importance—fighting will be intense. A lot of us won't be coming home, I suspect…

One of them—one of those not coming back—might be me. Guess it's up to the roll of the dice whether I make it through or not. I'm hopeful, but I've got to be truthful about my feelings, too.

Dearest, you know how much you mean to me, how much I love you. God, I miss you so much! Your eyes, your lips, your hair. I'd give anything just to touch you again, and smell your perfume…

When this crazy war is over—if and *when* I make it back—we can pick up where we left off… I'll become a doctor, just like Dad… then we can start our family…

Well, my stomach's rumbling so I'd better hit the chow line before it's too late. Big day tomorrow. There's scuttlebutt circulating that the General is supposed to visit tonight…

Lars says 'Hi'; says he feels like he knows you, I talk about you so much! Hope you two can meet when we're all back home…

Anyway, I'm signing off with tons of love

and kisses for you, darling.

Your devoted husband,

Ivan

The same day he sent the letter to Emilie, he received one from her. At last! And just in time…

He held off opening it for hours: just kept smelling it over and over, remembering her face, savoring the music of her voice, reminiscing about the warmth of her next to him…

Ivan's heart trip-hammered his body, threatening to burst through his chest wall at any moment like an internal grenade; his mouth was parched, his hands were shaking and his ears ached. The deafness amplified all of his other senses: taste, touch, sight, smell. His head was spinning, and his blood pressure was low, making everything jittery, strange. Artillery smoke rose in billowing, acrid clouds, the reek of sulfur, sweat, and guts riding the thermals with it. He found it difficult to concentrate through the vertigo, the nausea, the haze.

The C.O. was right: If he stayed where he was, he'd die as surely as the men around him were dying… *As surely as Lars had died… I can make this! I* will *make this!*

Even though he couldn't hear them, bullets sang and hissed like swarms of deadly insects, kicking up sand all over the beach. Looking at the water, he noticed that scores of bodies were washing onto shore with the high tide, even as the first few of the living laid a tentative claim to the strand.

They're getting through! Diving for shelter in a crater that had been blasted into the ground, Ivan was startled by another young soldier who appeared beside him, gripping his arm, shouting over the roar of bombs and gunfire that he could no longer hear.

Firing some rounds at their attackers, the soldier—probably no more than nineteen—was oddly touching as tears cleaned a path down his grimy cheeks. In a flash he stood, running from the scant cover Ivan had secured: A few seconds later, Ivan watched as a mortar round silently cut the boy in two…

Ivan passed out.

He had grown to be good pals with a long-boned soldier named Lars. They were two of a kind: From the same little town in the middle of nowhere, though they had never met before being assigned to their squadron. Lars had a way of making him laugh with his quirky sense of humor and spot-on voice impressions of popular singers and actors: The guy was a born mimic. They had spent many an evening cutting up when they should have been sleeping: Doing impersonations, talking about girls, dreaming aloud about going back home…

Once, they had even been able to take leave together and had gotten into a lot of trouble—things they'd never divulge to their wives or girlfriends. Fun times; memorable times; times that relieved the anguish of lost friends—which they had been forbidden to have, officially; times that eased the loneliness and helplessness they felt over dying parents, old acquaintances, distant lovers…

> Ivan—
>
> These words are really hard to write. Harder than any words I've ever written before. But I have to tell you the truth.
>
> I'm divorcing you; I'm in love with another man.
>
> Now you know. I'm so sorry to tell you this—you're such a good person and don't deserve this…
>
> I met him at the factory. He's a foreman in my department.

> We didn't mean to fall in love; it just happened. I still have affection and care about you, but he has to come first in my life; I can't deny the love we share for one another any longer…
>
> Just forget me. You deserve a better wife than me, and I really hope you find her. Please, try not to hate…
>
> Take good care of yourself. You will always be important in my life: my first true love.
>
> Goodbye,
> Emilie

Her letter was a bombshell. Ivan's breath was shallow, his body shaking.

I waited for hours to read—this? *From the highlight of my life to the lowest point on the same day… Why did she choose now to write her damn letter, just when I'm about to embark on my most dangerous assignment yet?*

He crumpled the note up in his fist, as if that could erase her painful words from his mind. Of course, she hadn't known about his mission: he'd sent the letter just today. Her message was post-dated three weeks ago.

A foreman, huh? Probably some rich guy… Probably better-looking than me. Probably show you a real fine time… You two'll be living the fucking highlife while I'm here getting my ass shot off…

His rage had nowhere to go except inward; he lay down in his bunk and cried, hoping that Lars wouldn't drop by…

The invaders were moving targets…

Big gun and artillery shells fell on the troops flooding the beach in a deadly rain; huge cannons delivered a continual barrage of devastation. Machine-gun, tank, and rifle fire cut the enemy down like stalks of wheat under a scythe. The groups that were able to crawl past the enemy line to the mortar craters at the base of the cliffs huddled there, pressing against the rocks, frozen with fear. Awake again, Ivan just stared, firing his weapon, when it occurred to him, from his makeshift shelter.

Sensing something behind him, Ivan looked back: Several other men had joined him. It was the colonel: he was shouting. The C.O.'s contorted face was sweaty and streaked with blood, his arm in a crude sling. His voice barely rose above the din, but Ivan could only read his lips: *"We can't stay here! The artillery will home in on us!"*

"Where do we go, sir? They've got us pinned down!" a recruit next to Ivan screamed over the bombardment. The sun was high in the sky now, a blazing eyeball watching dispassionately. The hours passed like seconds in some ways, years in others. The C.O. was about to answer when a ricochet slammed into his eye: he slumped over as the other men recoiled in silent horror.

Out of frustration more than fear, Ivan scrambled up a cliff, clawing at the dirt. Once on the modest summit, he realized how exposed he was and crouched down, bringing his rifle up. That was when he saw an enemy soldier watching him, his weapon already raised. The man screamed something in a foreign language: Ivan realized that it had to be, because he couldn't understand the lip movements. They were face to face, just a few yards apart as the man rushed toward him. Ivan was still holding his rifle in front of him; in a desperate move, he lunged at the other soldier, driving his bayonet hard into the man's chest. A gout of dark red blood shot from the astonished man's mouth, hitting Ivan in the face like a torrent of hot tar.

Ivan stared into the enemy's startled eyes, oblivious to the crush of the world around them. The youth gasped for air, a gory froth coating his lower jaw. He tried to speak, but Ivan couldn't read his bloody lips. The trooper clutched Ivan's rifle barrel, then reached forward, his crimson fingers smearing the blood on Ivan's face; he made a few more steps—impaling himself further—before falling over.

The soldier lay on the ground, unmoving: His glazed eyes stared skyward, devoid of life. Ivan sank to his knees, bile etching his throat. *How many of these same terrible moments are playing out here today?* Ivan's quiet world was all-consuming, and the dead man's eyes seemed to accuse him from the outskirts of eternity. At last he stood up, ready to move on, to fight, determined now more than ever to live. Looking down at the man a final time, he said, "I'm sorry—"

That was when he felt something at both legs, below the knees. The ground was giving way; he was losing his foothold … Then—

Riveting
waves of
pain …

He woke up that night to a cold and silent world. Eyes adjusting to the dark, Ivan realized that there was another man close to him, sharing refuge in the crater they were occupying … Ivan felt confused … thirsty … his lips were burning … On the horizon, he detected flashes of gunfire and large shell explosions. The battle was moving away from them … He slipped into unconsciousness …

He awoke at dawn, asking: "Have we been on the summit for hours or days?" Before his compatriot could answer, Ivan passed out again …

Awakening once more, Ivan stared at his new friend, finally able to see him clearly in the daylight. The man had once been an enemy, but was harmless now: His entire face was burned away, just a grinning, blackened skull, charred skin dangling in tatters, its teeth glinting in the hot sun.

Ivan peered out to the sea: The beach was theirs. He smiled… Nothing mattered now.

He collapsed into the comforting darkness again.

She was dressed in black, with a fancy box hat: Beautiful, just as he remembered her. She seemed genuinely delighted to see him. She took his hand in hers, sitting next to his bed. Emilie…

"Ivan, I was so worried you wouldn't make it home."

He stared at her, having regained some of his hearing. A slow process, his right ear was much improved, though the hearing in his left was still only a fraction of what it was before the injury. "Your letter didn't help," he said finally, avoiding her eyes as he pulled his hand away.

She was undeterred. "I hated having to write what I did, but… " Her voice faltered.

"Your timing was great," he said. "Where's the foreman?"

"He's home—with the baby."

"Baby?" *That actually shocked him:* My *baby?*

"I-I discovered I was pregnant right after I wrote you that last letter… "

"How nice," he said flatly, bewildered.

"You don't seem very glad to see me, Ivan," she said, eyes pleading, hands knotted. His smile was cold. Turning his head to the window, he noticed that it was getting dark. Closing his eyes, Ivan couldn't resist inhaling her perfume one last time.

"That's because I'm not,*" he said, still facing away. His eyes welled. "How could I be? You married him before the ink was dry on our divorce papers."*

"I thought… " Her face flushed. He was secretly glad that his damaged ear was the one facing her.

She continued: "I-I thought that… maybe… maybe we could be friends—"

Ivan snapped his gaze to hers, tears tracking his face: "You… *you thought wrong…"*

Emilie looked down, sniffling quietly. The air was bloated, the room suffocating. Then: "Were… were you badly hurt?"

"Bad enough." He gruffly pushed aside the blanket at his waist.

Her breath caught in her chest. She looked in his eyes: "Your legs… *"*

"That's right… Left 'em back on the beach, Emilie… Back on the beach with Lars. Bad enough what we lost; bad enough about Lars; bad enough what happened to me—though I'm luckier than most… But what you *did…" His face was an icy mask of anger. "What* you *did—that was the worst…"*

She stared at his mutilated body in horror. "I-I'm so sorry…"

He huffed, pulling the sheet back over himself. "I don't want your pity. *Just get the hell out of here and* never *come back."*

She looked at him, crying freely now, but his hardened face broke her; she gathered her purse, looking to the floor as she stood. "Goodbye, Ivan."

He watched the door close behind her, then turned his head to the window again. It had started to rain. He closed his eyes.

"Even though it's over, it never really ends…"

I'm a Batman freak. I've lived his adventures since high school in Missouri. The beginning of this story reflects that passion. Fun! *But then it turns much darker.*

—WFN

A LOT LIKE THE JOKER

Yeah, yeah, he had him now, by golly! Had him in a really neat chokehold. No matter how much he tried, he couldn't break the hold. His eyes were all bugged and his tongue was sticking out and that big red mouth of his was way open, gasping for air.

The question is: Why doesn't Batman finish him for good? Why let him go on living and committing fresh crimes?

If he's thrown back into Arkham Asylum he'll just escape like he always does and then Batman will have to go catch him all over again. Stupid! Just frigging kill him!

Disgusted, Jimmy Loving tossed the comic book aside. Even if it was the first all-Joker issue (big collector's item) and required delicate handling, Jimmy was too frustrated to care. He'd lost respect for Batman. The caped crusader was a flake.

Jimmy was certain of one thing though—if he were Batman he would have killed the Joker years ago. He sat back in his seat, staring through the bus window at the passing late-day landscape. It would be sundown soon, after the next rest stop, and by early morning, they'd be pulling into Chicago where his father would meet him for a whole summer of fun.

My third summer with Pop. No more chores for mother back at the farm in Kansas. I hate Kansas, all flat and boring.

He guessed he hated his mother, too, but he wasn't sure. Whenever she was high on drugs, she wanted to hug him and got all sloppy and sentimental. He hated her then for sure. He used to jump out the back window of his bedroom when he heard her coming home, giggling foolishly, and singing off-key the way she did when she was stoned.

He also hated his family name. *The Loving family. What a crock!* Jimmy was glad that his father and mother had divorced three years ago when he was nine. His father had moved to Chicago (fun city!) where Jimmy got to spend each summer. *Super cool.* All he had in Kansas was a couple of loopy school friends (and school sucked) and his comic book collection.

Now that he'd decided that Batman was a jerk he figured to go for Captain America. He was a lot tougher than Batman, and Jimmy liked the way he handled his big round shield. Boy, Cap could really sling that thing! *Pow! Wap!*

The bus rumbled past a gaudy adult theater with HOT AND SEXY lettered on the marquee, and Jimmy told himself: *I gotta learn all about sex.* Maybe his father could tell him about it in Chicago now that Jimmy was twelve.

Last year one of his loopy friends had given him a magazine with photos of naked ladies in it, but he never had a chance to look it over before his mother found the magazine in his bedroom and threw it into the trash. She was pissed that he had it. Then there was the time he'd been invited to a "spin-the-bottle" party. It was tremendously thrilling when the bottle pointed to him and he got to kiss Mary Ellen Baker in the kitchen. It was really dark there so he couldn't see her face, but he was pretty sure it was Mary Ellen Baker.

There were rumors at school about Homer Jackson, who played terrific basketball, that he'd once made a girl come by sucking her toes, but Jimmy had his doubts about the truth of this rumor, and Homer Jackson never talked about sex. He just grinned a lot.

Jimmy felt very adult, traveling to Chicago on his own. (Up to now his mother had taken him to see his father, but this time he'd insisted on traveling alone.) He'd soon be fully grown, tall and strong like his father, who was a six-footer. A real man. Adulthood was scary, but Jimmy looked forward to it.

When the bus stopped at a railroad crossing Jimmy watched a very thin dog, obviously a stray, limp slowly across the tracks. Jimmy could count all his ribs and his patched fur was mottled.

When I get rich I'll donate a lot of my money to animal charities because animals need to be treated just like other people. He felt the same way about fish. *They shouldn't be pulled out of the water with a barbed steel hook in their mouth.* He remembered, as a little boy, going to a fish hatchery with his mother and seeing, in one room, a bunch of awful men who were banging living fish against the wall, smashing them to death. *How could anybody do that?* Jimmy never forgot.

Jimmy liked to think about being rich. His father was not rich, but made pretty darn good money as a fire insurance adjuster in Chicago. A good city for his father because Chicago had a lot of fires. That's why he moved there from Kansas—for the fires.

Jimmy figured he would play the stock market and make a fortune although he knew nothing about the stock market. When he first heard about it, he thought it was a market for livestock. Or maybe a really big grocery store. Jimmy's grandma (on his Mom's side) gave him a dollar on his birthday and a dollar at Christmas. She claimed that when she was a little girl her father gave her a dollar on holidays and that you could buy a *lot* for a dollar. It did no good to point out, as Jimmy tried to do, that today's dollar doesn't buy much of anything.

Stuff costs a lot more now than when grandma was a little girl, but she never understood that. Heck, just last week Jimmy had to pay three bucks for one chocolate bar.

The bus wasn't crowded. Two old ladies. A lanky cowboy in a white Stetson. A bearded rabbi and …

… another boy a little older than Jimmy seated across from him. Mohawk haircut, long, skinny, arms, lots of tattoos. (Even on his neck there was a coiled dragon.) He was dressed in ragged jeans and a stained t-shirt bearing the words "I am a slave." His belt buckle featured a grinning skull. The boy lit a thin brown cigar.

"You're not supposed to smoke on the bus," Jimmy told him.

"Fuck the bus," the boy said. He puffed out a thin cloud of cigar smoke.

"It's against the rules," said Jimmy.

"Fuck the rules. I make my own rules."

"What's your name?"

"Why you wanna know?"

"Just curious." Jimmy extended his right hand across the aisle. "I'm Jimmy Loving."

The boy sullenly ignored the outthrust hand. "What kinda sappy name is that?"

Jimmy nodded. "I know. I hate it. All the kids at school make fun of it."

"It's a sappy name," the boy said, drawing on his cigar.

"You going to Chicago?" asked Jimmy. "My pop is gonna meet me in Chicago."

"Fuck Chicago. I'm getting off at Crestvale."

"Is that a town?"

"Damn right and it sure beats Chicago ten ways from Sunday."

"You ever been to Chicago?" asked Jimmy.

"Sure, I been there a couple of times. Scored a neat set of caps there last summer. Sold 'em for prime coin."

"Caps?"

"Hubcaps, dummy! I jacked a neat set in Chi. Off a new Caddie."

"That's against the law."

"Fuck the law," said the boy.

The bus was slowing.

"Here's where I split."

The boy stepped down from the bus. As the door hissed closed Jimmy noticed a large sign arching over the street:

WELCOME TO CRESTVALE
The Little Town with a Big Heart

Jimmy shrugged. *Never did get his name. Boy, he was really tough-talking! Mom hates to hear kids swear. She whupped me raw when I used the F-word once…*

One by one, the other passengers left the bus as it made more stops. First, the two old ladies, then the cowboy and the rabbi, leaving Jimmy alone in his seat as thick darkness descended like a velvet shroud from the moon-clouded sky. Towns flickered past in a blur of neon lights as the heavy vehicle rolled on toward Chicago.

I oughta try and get some shuteye, Jimmy told himself. *Still a lotta hours before I see Pop.*

He was just nodding off when the bus jolted heavily over a section of rough terrain. Jimmy peered out of the window. They were off the main highway on a narrow dirt road that cut through thick woods.

"Hey," Jimmy hailed the driver. "How come we left the highway? Is something wrong?"

"Don't worry, kid. Everything's fine." The driver still

faced away from Jimmy. Big shoulders. Thick neck. The man shut down the engine.

A deep-night silence.

"Where are we?" asked Jimmy.

"Never mind where we are," growled the heavy-set man.

It was really hot inside the bus. *Maybe the heater is messed up.* Outside the window, thunder cracked, and rain tears began running down the glass. Jimmy flinched at another cannon burst. "Why have we stopped?"

The bus driver chuckled. "I got my reasons," he said, and turned toward the boy. The vehicle's ceiling lights sliced his face into sharp, unpleasant angles.

Jimmy was startled. "Wow! You look a lot like ... the Joker."

The driver had a beaked nose, a pointed chin, very pale skin, and a scary red-lipped mouth.

"I'm no joker, kid," he said, "I'm something else."

"Oh? What ... What are you?"

"You'll find out." And the big man was smiling as he left his seat and walked slowly down the bus aisle toward the boy.

Jimmy Loving felt, suddenly, very cold.

WITH THE DARK GUY

A Conversation

BOB ATTICUS: Hi! In case you just tuned in, you are listening to KBZ Radio, and I'm your host, Bob Atticus. We have a special treat for you. We are bringing you an exclusive live interview with a truly amazing gentleman. Yes, folks, our guest tonight is none other than Mr. Death himself, who is sitting right across from me here in the studio. [ebullient] Welcome, sir!

MR.DEATH: Thanks, Bob! Great to be with you.

ATTICUS: As I understand it, this is your first public interview.

DEATH: Right-o. I'm kinda shy. Like to stay in the background. I'm really an introvert.

ATTICUS: So you're… reclusive.

DEATH: Well, I never push myself into the limelight.

ATTICUS: Since this is not TV, would you care to describe yourself for our listening audience?

DEATH: Oh, sure . . . ! Uh, I'm all in black. Never wear anything else. I carry a scythe. Black cowl over my face. Wear sunglasses, and am very thin.

ATTICUS: I can see that you are almost skeletal. Just how much do you weigh?

DEATH: It varies. When a large bunch of people die, I tend to gain weight. This has been a slow month . . . so I'm down to about 120.

ATTICUS: Hmmm . . . for a six-footer, that's pretty slim.

DEATH: Yeah, I know. [sighs] But until more folks buy the farm . . .

ATTICUS: Switching subjects . . . I've often wondered about something. Do you eat people?

DEATH: My goodness, no! Never! I'm no cannibal, Bob. I just make sure their heart stops . . . that they're dead meat.

ATTICUS: I must confess, sir, that many people consider you to be evil.

DEATH: Gosh, that's nutty! I'm just pragmatic. Folks have to die, and my job is to see that they do. Nothing evil about it.

ATTICUS: You certainly seem to be a jolly-good fella. [hesitates] I'm curious and have to ask . . . Why did you agree to this interview?

DEATH: To set the record straight. To make my position clear. To snuff rumors about me being some kind of evil son of a bitch… Uh… can we say "bitch" on the air?

ATTICUS: No problem. I gotta say—to me, you sure seem like a really nice guy.

DEATH: Hey, Bob… that's very kind of you to say. Thank you for the compliment. [chuckles] I don't get many.

ATTICUS: That's because you're frightening to most people. Hard for them to warm up to you.

DEATH: [lightly] I'm like a lizard—cold-blooded!

ATTICUS: I need some clarification on the Black Plague… same goes for the Spanish Inquisition and the Holocaust.

DEATH: Just what do you need to know?

ATTICUS: Well, they were all pretty horrible. Did they make you feel guilty?

DEATH: Shucks, no! I'm just a transfer man.

ATTICUS: What do you mean by that?

DEATH: I transfer 'em from life to me. That's my job.

ATTICUS: By the way, how old are you? Seems like you've been around for quite a spell.

DEATH: You got that right. I'm… oh… at least thousands of years old, millions probably. I never celebrate my birthday anymore. Too depressing.

ATTICUS: I have to ask: Are *you* ever going to die?

DEATH: Well, I'll be here till the last living thing is up Salt Creek. [chuckles] That's slang for being deceased. Gonna take a while. After that, who the heck knows?

ATTICUS: What about your parents? Do you have a Mom and Dad?

DEATH: Not that I know of. If I did, they'd sure both be dead by now.

ATTICUS: I appreciate your candor.

DEATH: Always try to tell the truth.

ATTICUS: Do you have special powers? I mean, could you *keep* people from dying?

DEATH: Now, why would I do that? Be out of a job. Even if I *could* save people, I'd be a sap to do it.

ATTICUS: I see what you mean.

DEATH: I listen to your program whenever you report on disasters. You know, like volcanic eruptions, major earthquakes, sudden floods—stuff like that.

ATTICUS: Do you cause these things?

DEATH: No way! I'm just there when they happen.

ATTICUS: And you never feel even a tinge of guilt—about what you do?

DEATH: No siree, not a tinge! I'm proud of the job I do. Golly, Bob, I'm doing a public service for zillions of people. I do what I can to help keep things in balance.

ATTICUS: Do you kill animals, too?

DEATH: Yep. Far as I'm concerned, every living thing has to go—grass, plants, insects—the works. Only natural.

ATTICUS: I gotta admit—you *are* pretty scary looking.

DEATH: So are clowns. Lotta people are shit-scared of clowns. [hesitates] Can we say "shit" on the air?

ATTICUS: They'll bleep it out. But dick, bastard, and ass are okay.

DEATH: Wow!

ATTICUS: Is there life after you? Do people go on in a different form?

DEATH: Nice to think so, but the answer is nope, dead is dead. Period.

ATTICUS: That's depressing to hear.

DEATH: I'm just telling it like it is.

ATTICUS: About your scythe … do you actually *use* it?

DEATH: Naw, It's just a trademark. [chuckles] Ole Death and his scythe.

ATTICUS: When did you start … doing what you do?

DEATH: It was back when Adam and Eve kicked the bucket.

ATTICUS: I don't mean to get personal, but … you really *do* need to put on some weight.

DEATH: Oh, I'll be fine. The Mideast looks very promising. Always seems to, lately. Violent uprisings are neat. And mass slaughter is always good.

ATTICUS: Do you have any favorite species relating to your job?

DEATH: I favor fruit flies. They die fast. Turtles are annoying. They take forever to kick off.

ATTICUS: I hear that Old Faithful, in Yellowstone, is actually a giant volcano due for a major eruption.

DEATH: Really? That's great news.

ATTICUS: Well, it's been a real pleasure … but I'm afraid our time is up.

DEATH: Hey, no sweat. I'm overdue at a fatal air crash. Plane hit a mountain in Colorado. I gotta make sure nobody survives.

ATTICUS: I really hate to cut this short, but we *are* out of time.

DEATH: No, Bob, not *we—you*.

ATTICUS: What do you mean?

DEATH: Remember that stroke you had last year?

ATTICUS: Of course. I was lucky to survive it.

DEATH: It weakened your heart, Bob. You asked me why I agreed to do this interview, and I told you.

ATTICUS: So?

DEATH: So I didn't tell you the *full* reason. [a moment of silence] I came here for you, Bob.

ATTICUS: For me? You mean …

DEATH: That's right.

ATTICUS: [alarmed tone] Are you telling me… that I'm *dead*?

DEATH: You will be in a moment.

ATTICUS: [gasping for breath] Uh… ah… ak… my *heart*!

DEATH: Sorry, but it's all over for you, Bob. [sound of Bob's body hitting the floor, covered by an uprush of music]

NEW HOST: Ladies and gentlemen, this concludes our interview for this evening. Stay tuned for a "golden oldie." [into: "As Time Goes By"]

[Piano up . . .]

Robotic life has always fascinated me. This story is a variation on this idea, which I have often tackled before, but not quite in this manner.

—WFN

A NEW MAN

[neuro-prom passcode: required
(press any key to enter)
passcode: ______________
passcode: accepted

unspooling … … … … … …
start transcode;!complete!
checksum … … … … … … … …

</gmd:linkage>
</gmd:ci onlineresource>
</geop:mappingfile>
<geop:processingapplication>
<geop:ph_environmentobject>
<geop:documentation>
<gmd:ci_onlineresource>
<gco:characterstring>geoserver wfs</gco:characterstring>
</geop:name>
<geop:purpose><gco:characterstring>produce representation
of observation datasets inscience modelling language—a
ghl-based application schema</gco:characterstring></

gmd:purpose>
<geop:type><gco:characterstring>software</
gco:characterstring></geop:type>
<geop:version><gco:characterstring>complex

run #tea3170b-x3075 transcription:>

"Happy tenth anniversary!" I said, handing the ribboned jewelry box to Edith.

"What's inside?" she asked, eyes aglow with excitement. She was still beautiful enough to astonish me.

"Open it and see," I said.

With a girlish laugh, she untied the red band and opened the box. She gasped.

"Well? Do you like it?"

"Terry! An emerald necklace! You shouldn't have. It must have cost—"

"I can afford it. Nothing's too good for my girl . . . " I've always called Edith "my girl," ever since we met in college. It was love at first sight for us both; I've never wanted another woman. Edith was my treasure.

She lifted the choker from its velvet nest and slipped it around her neck, allowing afternoon sunlight to turn the jewels to green fire.

"It's absolutely gorgeous!"

We kissed, deeply, with a sexual hunger that was still intense, consuming. After ten years, the excitement had not diminished.

We had our anniversary dinner at Jimmy's, our favorite Italian restaurant. It was named after actor James Cagney, and framed photos of the long-dead movie icon adorned the walls. In one photo Cagney was posing with President Franklin Roosevelt in the Oval Office during World War II.

Benny LaGarda, the owner, greeted us warmly, excited about a 1949 Cagney film he'd recently discovered, *White Heat.* He was rail-thin, with a short neck, and displayed an obvious over-bite when he smiled.

"The scene at the end is *fabulous*," he told us. "Jimmy gets blown to pieces! He's on this really high platform and he yells to his mother, 'Look, Ma—top of the world!', and that's when he's blown to bits!" He directed us to a table near the kitchen. "Too bad they didn't have our technology a hundred years ago, eh? Jimmy might have been saved."

"Mmmm," Edith murmured as she sat down, "smells delicious!" She had always enjoyed the heady aroma of Italian herbs and spices. She was wearing the necklace, the emeralds flashing green heat against the white of her throat.

"This is our tenth anniversary," I told Benny, squeezing my wife's hand, "so we want a bottle of your best champagne."

"Our treat," nodded Benny. "If I'd known about this happy occasion I would have baked a cake."

"The bubbly will do just fine," said Edith, smiling up at him. "Wow ... I haven't tasted champagne since we had Janette."

"Where *are* the children?" Benny asked.

"Janette loves shuttlefusion," said Edith. "The big game is tonight ... for the West Coast Championship, so we dropped off Jan and Bobby at the 'drome."

"Yeah." I nodded. "We needed time for just the two of us."

"Jan has a crush on one of the players," declared Edith. "I've forgotten his name. Lance something-or-other. But I'm sure it'll pass. She's only nine years old!"

"They grow up fast these days," said Benny, taking our order.

As always, the food was delicious: A sumptuous vegetarian feast prepared by Benny himself; the champagne was a perfect complement.

Later that evening we made passionate love; Edith could be a tiger in bed, especially on an occasion as special as our anniversary. Afterward, we had the car drive us to the Friodrome to pick up Jan and Bobby.

"How was the game?" I asked Bobby. At eight, he was easily bored.

He shrugged. "It was okay. Jannie's the shuttle freak, not me. But it was okay."

"It was *super!*" Jan declared. "Best game *ever!* And our team won, thanks to Lance. He was the star. He scored *three* times!"

"Kid's an air head," I said. "Dumb as a sack of rocks."

In the rearview, I saw her chin quiver as she looked away. The silence was heavy.

"Now see what you've done," admonished Edith after a few moments. "A terrible thing to say when you don't even know the boy."

Janette finally blurted: "Daddy, you just don't understand true love!"

At the breakfast table the next morning, Bobby picked at his food, head down, looking glum.

"What's wrong, soldier?" I asked him.

"Why can't we program the table to make a different breakfast?"

"How different?"

"I'm tired of toast and soy bacon. I want a bowl of cereal."

"Now, you know we've had this discussion before. Those kids' cereals are full of sugar," Edith said, "Very bad for you. That's why we don't buy them."

"Look," I told him, "you are not old enough to dictate a menu yet. Later, when you're older and if you still want cereal we can discuss the matter. For now, *you* eat what *we* eat."

Bobby scowled. "Other kids can eat cereal." He stared at the food on his plate. He knew this was a losing battle.

"Well, you're not other kids," his mother replied, her expression stern as she dried her hands on a dishtowel. "Stop sulking, and don't waste your food. Children on Io are starving."

He looked at me. "How come all the *bad* stuff tastes better than the *good* stuff?"

I had no answer to that; I'd never figured it out either.

Everything went wrong after the crash.

I had set the auto-drive at near max; I enjoyed the sensation of sheer speed. The car was probably moving faster over the road slot than was prudent. But the slot was designed to keep all cars separated on the GridWay, so I felt safe, drowsing in my seat, eyes closed, picturing Edith's happy smile when I got back to our house-unit.

That's when the slot malfunctioned: As a heavy med truck moved toward me, it jumped the Grid and slammed head-on into my car. I learned later that the ensuing impact tore my body apart as the two machines merged in a horrific tangle of twisted metal. The man in the truck, amazingly, survived with only minor injuries.

I did not: I died in the hospital shortly after arrival. The minute I expired, they flashed my Neuro-prom and affected the dendritic transfer into my new host. I woke up several weeks after the operation flushed with strength, alert and in no pain.

"Welcome back to the land of the living," declared my white-clad doctor, smiling down at me. "The scan shows you're fit as a fiddle."

I blinked at him. "What happened? I don't understand ... "

"You were in an accident. Your old body didn't survive intact, but we were able to replicate your damaged mind and restore it into a new physique."

"Incredible. I feel great," I told him. "When can I ... I mean, am I free to leave?"

"In a few more days ... There is some neuro-finalization to complete now that you've been taken out of induced coma. Mostly hippocampus re-integration and amygdala testing. Once that's done, you may go home." He was quiet, only looking down once to make a notation. "As to expectations once you get back, you might be a little unsteady, and have sporadic memory leaks—even some false ones—for the next few months until the imaging is fully absorbed into your recovered Neuro-prom. The organic/holographic mind interface takes time to fully mesh. Other than that, I think you will mend physically in a few more weeks."

I considered all of this, still overwhelmed. "I feel like a new man."

"In a very real sense, that's exactly what you are. Many of your body parts have been replaced. In fact, your synths are superior to the originals. Once you finish healing, I believe you'll be pleased with the final result."

"I owe you, doctor," was the best reply I could manage. "Is my wife here?"

He nodded. "Mrs. Airth is in the waiting room. I'll send for her." He turned to leave, pausing at the door. "Have a good, new life, Mr. Airth."

Settled comfortably in the back seat of the new slot car as it hummed smoothly along the Grid, I asked Edith how the kids had reacted to my accident.

"Let's not talk about the children now," she said, pursing her lips in the familiar pout that I found so erotic. "I've rented a wonderful lux-unit just for the two of us in the New Bahamas—a perfect place to celebrate our tenth anniversary."

"But that was weeks ago," I said.

"Then call it a post-celebration," she murmured, kissing me on the neck. Her lips were warm, and her right leg pressed firmly against mine. I was pleased when my new body responded instantly; Edith was a very passionate woman.

The ride back to our place proved to be a memorable one.

At home, Edith had the Wallbar produce two French Martinis. "Here's to your homecoming, darling!" she said, raising her glass.

The drink was strong, and I felt slightly dizzy. Noticing my flushed appearance, she looked concerned.

"Did the doctor say it was all right for you to drink?"

"Oh, sure," I declared. "No problem. Let's have another."

"No *way*. You need to take it easy after all this trauma. He told me about the memory leaks, the mental re-integration."

I protested, telling her I was fine, but she insisted. Changing the subject, I asked: "Where are the kids?"

"I left them with my sister. They do love their Aunt Laura."

My new mind blanked on the name. "I want to talk to them. Let's call over there."

Edith shook her head as she took a sip of her drink. "You know how eccentric she is. Remember how much she hates vidcalls? She never answers. But don't worry, she's good with the kids."

I regarded her a moment, confused. "Okay, but I miss them. At least we can call and leave a message. Let them know I'm going to be fine."

"I told them you were away on a business trip. I didn't want them to know about your accident until we were sure you were going to be all right. They'll be okay until we get back."

"Back? From where?"

She smiled. "I've rented a wonderful lux-unit in the New Bahamas, remember? Nassau—just for the two of us. You'll love it!"

She was right. I *did* love it in Nassau. It was like a second honeymoon. But I missed Jan and Bobby; something seemed wrong. The night of our return home, I found Aunt Laura's number in Edith's cell and called her as she prepared dinner.

"What are you talking about? I haven't seen those kids in ages. *Aren't they with you?*"

"I need to talk to Edith," and I broke the connection.

I confronted my wife, my face tight. "*Where* are Jan and Bobby?"

She looked at me, surprised at my intensity. "Promise not to be upset if I tell you?"

I stared at her. "Go on."

"The children are in a better place." She took my hand in hers. "This world is *not* for children."

I glared at her. My head was pounding. "My *God*, woman! What have you done with our children?" My fists were balled.

"I … dispatched them. It was quick … painless … "

I couldn't form words; my throat was locked. Finally: "*You killed our children?*" I was shaking.

"I removed them from a violent, hostile world.

They're … at peace now. Their bodies are resting in the backyard."

A wave of red rage swept over me and I lost all control, lunging toward her. Fastening my fingers around her throat, I squeezed as hard as I could. She tried to scream, twisting frantically to free herself as my thumbs sank deep into her neck.

It wasn't long before she stopped moving.

"… and that's why I'm here … to confess to the murder of my wife."

The officer behind the high desk blinked at me, dark eyes wide. "Look, mister, I'm only a sergeant. Let me get Lieutenant Forbes."

"Fine," I told him. "I'll wait."

Lieutenant Forbes, serious, thin-faced, and balding, appeared in due course. "What's the problem?"

"This guy," the officer said, pointing at me; the cadence of his voice was tense. "Says he offed his old lady. Come in to confess."

"I'm guilty," I told the Lieutenant. "You can put me in cuffs." I extended my wrists.

He waved dismissively. "We don't handcuff people until we have a reason."

"Well, I'm a murderer. Isn't that reason enough?"

"Where's your wife now?"

"She's dead, back at our home-unit. She killed our children. Said they're buried in the backyard."

The officer put his hand up. "I'll have to check all this out Mister … "

"… Airth. Terence Eugene Airth."

"Just sit down, Mr. Airth, 'til I get a full report."

I took a chair by the window and waited.

They found Edith and the children just as I said they

would: My confession was confirmed as completely accurate. They dug up two small bodies in the backyard as well, and DNA samples confirmed that it was Bobby and Jan. The investigation about what had happened to our children would require more time to research.

I was placed into a holding cell.

A week later, Forbes unlocked my cell door. "You're free to go, Mr. Airth. We have no reason to hold you. Apologies for the delay, but we had to be sure that you hadn't killed the children, and the only way was a complete Neural Recovery of your wife's mind data."

"But … what I did to Edith … "

"No." The officer shook his head. "You're not guilty of a crime."

"But … that's *crazy!*"

"It's very simple, Mr. Airth. The investigation revealed that your wife had undergone a change, a major transformation." He paused. "Look, we checked—it happened while you were in the induced coma."

"*What* happened?" I blinked at him. "What are you talking about?"

"Your wife was a *machine* Mr. Airth; there is no law against the shutdown, however violent, of a machine."

My voice wavered. "Edith was … "

"A Simuloid Mark 6. What we pieced together was that after your accident, your wife suffered a massive stroke at the news; they used the Simuloid Procedure to offset the stroke, which had completely paralyzed her and put her into a vegetative state."

My mind was reeling. "But why didn't they opt to give her the Neuro-prom reconfiguration like I had?"

Forbes shook his head. "No way to do it. The stroke had destroyed her brain. She wasn't a candidate for that.

The murder of your children was a software failure after her Mindmap was degraded by the data cloning procedure."

"But she was so real, so lifelike." I ran my hand through my hair. "So … when I … did what I did to her … it was a machine killing … a *machine?*"

The lieutenant smiled. "The Mark 6 is an excellent product, but it's not perfect. It's still a replicant." Forbes rubbed his face, sensing my confusion. "See, you're not a machine, Mr. Airth. Even though your body parts were largely replaced, because your mind was simulated *perfectly* from your healthy brain to the Neuro-prom, you maintained your … *humanity*.

"On the other hand, your wife's body *and* brain were totally robotic; since her Mindbuild was incomplete and damaged by the stroke, the doctors were forced into manual reconstruction Safe Mode from her Historychip backup. Unfortunately, the backup had bad sectors that were missed in the cluster verification process … In other words, her NeuralOS was corrupted, which is why she malfunctioned with the children … I'm very sorry for your loss."

<END CONFESSION #TEA3170B-X3075
TRANSCRIPTION:

Compiling … … … … … … …..
!complete!
Checksum … … … … … … … … …..

</gmd:linkage>
</gmd:CI OnlineResource>
</geop:mappingFile>
<geop:processingApplication>
<geop:PH_EnvironmentObject>

<geop:documentation>
<gmd:CI_OnlineResource>
<gco:CharacterString>GeoServer WFS</
gco:CharacterString>
</geop:name>
<geop:purpose><gco:CharacterString>produce
representation of observation datasets in Modelling
Language—a GHL-based application schema</
gco:CharacterString></gmd:purpose>
<geop:type><gco:CharacterString>Software</
gco:CharacterString></geop:type>
<geop:version><gco:CharacterString>Complex

Encryption Complete.

CLOSE #TEA3170B-X3075 DOCUMENT UPLINK]

Do you believe in the supernatural? What about the cosmic? Well, in this story, Philip Dexter is on your side. He's convinced himself that it's a lot of nonsense. However…

Read "Like a Dead Man Walking": decide for yourself if dead men do *walk.*

—WFN | JVB

LIKE A DEAD MAN WALKING

In a lonely house near the heart of L.A., a phone rang.
"Hello?"

"Dex, Sanford Evans here. Listen: have you heard about that dead girl the police found in Bel Air? Not too far from you. It's all over the TV and Internet … "

"Afraid I haven't been watching the news," Philip Dexter replied. He was in his early thirties, a strong-boned man whose only vice was smoking. Lighting a cigarette, he frowned in self-disgust, then stubbed it out on a desk ashtray.

"Well, it's a real strange situation, Dex. Chief of Police gave an interview claiming that the washed-out skin and collapsed, sack-like appearance of the girl's body was the result of *exsanguination:* The body had been totally drained of blood, but—here's the kicker—Coroner said there were no serious injuries. Like it was sucked right out of her." There was a beat of silence over the line. "The speculation made me think of you."

Dexter cleared his throat. "I can guess what the 'speculation' was all about … "

"So guess, Dex."

"The undead, am I right?"

"You win the magic prize, Dex! There's been a *lot* of zombie talk—"

"All of which is horseshit!" Philip himself was surprised by the virulence of his declaration. Calmer: "That's what I'm debunking in my book—all the ... misconceptions."

"Easy, Dex! Just thought you should know about it ... Speaking as your publisher, how's your little opus coming along?"

Philip snorted into the handset; he detested it when people called him Dex, but he needed this book deal. "I'm well into it. Been working from a ton of notes. Gonna be an eye-opener." He looked at the clock, feeling the urge to get back to work.

"Excellent. We'll need the manuscript here in New York by mid-January at the latest: Can you swing that, Dex?" Evans' voice had an edge; the two men rarely spoke, and Philip had the feeling that Evans didn't really take him or his work seriously.

"No problem. Got it all set up in my mind. Nothing like it since Houdini."

"That's my man! Can't wait to read it. We'll target it for a spring release. Have a good day, Dex." The line went dead.

Philip put the phone down and walked to a large picture window facing the ocean. The wind was up and heavy waves were riding onto the beach, spilling lines of white froth along the sand. The sky was slate-gray, totally devoid of clouds. Turning away, he walked into the den, thinking about having a cigarette. "Gotta quit," he muttered.

The recently purchased Malibu home was still largely unfurnished: Crates of unpacked books lined the walls, scattered furniture and some boxes littered the unlit rooms. Philip Dexter sat down to a bright computer screen; he hesitated, organizing his thoughts, then began dancing his fingers across the keys.

Why is it that otherwise intelligent, clear-minded people continue to believe in the supernatural? Things such as ghosts, zombies, and vampires? There is no rational basis for such bizarre belief. It's time to expose the phonies who bilk millions each year out of gullible victims; time to go after the fake seers, bogus fortune tellers and trick mystics…

Philip checked a notebook entry, nodded to himself, and resumed typing:

Harry Houdini exposed countless fake mediums in the last century—the glowing face which he proved to be a dummy's head… the ghost of an old woman's dead son who turned out to be the medium's own kid in a weird getup… the floating trumpet on wires…

The phone jangled at his elbow, and he eased back from the screen to answer the call. "Yes?"

"Is this Philip Dexter?"

"Speaking. What can I do for you?"

"I'm Evelyn Court, the wife of Alex Court."

"The sculptor who died of a heart attack last month? My condolences on your loss. I enjoyed his work."

The woman hesitated. "I—I heard about your forthcoming book, and I need help from someone who understands… the supernatural."

"You've got the wrong guy, Mrs. Court. With all due respect, I'm into proving that it's just superstition and nonsense."

"No." Another pause. "No, I assure you, Mr. Dexter: It's all *real,* but… the police refuse to believe me."

"About what?"

"About the fact that my husband is… *alive.*"

"What a second … His funeral made headlines. And now you're saying—"

"Alex *hated* me!" she blurted out. "He blamed *me* for trying to destroy his career. Out of jealousy! Because he was famous and I wasn't." Her tone was intense. "It's not true! I was never, *ever* jealous of his success. I loved him, Mr. Dexter … But, time and again, we got into terrible rows over it. And … and he *threatened* me … "

"Threatened you how?"

"To … to *kill* me, Mr. Dexter." Philip could hear the tremor in her voice. "And … and I'm afraid *he will!*"

Philip was shocked into a momentary silence.

"Dead men don't kill people, Mrs. Court. And they sure don't come back to life! I'm not the guy to talk to. I suggest you see a shrink. Sounds to me like you need professional help."

"No—I need to see *you!* If you'll just meet me I know that I can convince you that what I fear is *real.*"

Philip thought for a moment, idly playing with a paperclip. "I'll admit you've made me curious. Maybe you'll end up in my book."

"Then you *will* meet me?"

Philip laughed. "When and where?"

Evelyn Court was full-figured, attractive, with nervous eyes and a tight, thin-lipped mouth. She sat uneasily on a red leather couch in her Bel Air home, twisting a scarf in her hands as she talked.

"Two nights ago, I thought that I heard a sound … So I went out to my husband's studio—the first time since his death—to check on a gallery sculpture for a client … " Fear radiated from her eyes. "As soon as I stepped inside he was there … standing in the shadows … glaring at me."

"Who? Who was there, Mrs. Court?" Philip asked.

"Alex … It was Alex."

"Are you saying that you saw Alexander Court's ghost?"

"No, not a ghost, Mr. Dexter. He was there … in the flesh."

"How can you be sure it wasn't an intruder?" Philip was scribbling notes into a worn notepad.

She shook her head. "No, Mr. Dexter, it was Alex, my husband. When he stepped into the beam from my flashlight, I saw him clearly. He had a sculpting knife in his hand … "

Philip looked up. "What did you do?"

"I—I ran back to the house and locked myself inside. Then I called the police—but since there was no sign of a break-in they thought I was—"

"Delusional?"

"Something like that." She got up, paced the room. "After the police left I couldn't sleep. I kept hearing noises from the studio, but I wasn't *about* to go back in there."

"Could be an animal. A raccoon maybe."

Mrs. Court gave a strained smile. "I think he was there again … in the studio."

Philip lit a cigarette.

"Please … I ask you not to smoke."

"Sorry," he said, hastily stubbing out the cigarette. "Lousy habit. I've been trying to quit."

She stared at him. "You're like the police … You don't believe me, do you—about seeing Alex?"

He rubbed his forehead, thinking. "I believe that you saw an *intruder*—even one who may have looked like your late husband."

She moved to a desk drawer and picked up a small flashlight. "I can prove what I say is true if you'll come with me."

Reluctantly, Philip followed her as she crossed the rear yard toward a marble edifice at the edge of the property: A family crypt. The late afternoon sun cast long tree shadows over the ornate entry door, which was adorned by two marble angels.

"Alex had this built when we bought the house three years ago," she said, pushing open the heavy door. "He loathed the idea of being buried in open earth ... so we placed his coffin here, according to his wishes ... He created the door sculpture himself."

Philip was impressed with the sumptuous craftsmanship. "Amazing: quite a talented man."

She continued: "At first, I think he truly loved me ... " She took a step inside. "But then ... " Her voice trailed off as she probed the gloom with the flashlight, illuminating a portion of marble wall. Under the bright beam, Philip was able to read the chiseled inscription:

ALEXANDER EDWARD COURT
Rest in Peace

Evelyn slid back the marble facing and pulled Alex Court's bronze coffin from its slot. "Go ahead," she said to Philip. "Open it. See for yourself."

Philip tipped back the lid as she directed the torch beam to reveal the silk-lined interior.

The coffin was empty.

"*Now* are you satisfied. Mr. Dexter?"

Philip sighed. "Afraid not. The way I read it, this intruder, whoever he is, wants you to believe your husband is alive. I think he removed Court's body from this crypt ... "

"What possible reason would anyone have to perpetrate such an awful hoax?"

"I don't have an answer for that," he replied.

"I think Madame Jechiel has something to do with this..."

"Who is Madame Jechiel?" Philip continued to scribble in his notepad.

"She owns a gallery on La Cienega. I arranged for a showing of my husband's work there about three weeks before he died. She has a strong belief in the... occult."

"So do lots of misguided people," Philip said. He looked back into the coffin. "I don't see any connection."

"Alex was *terrified* of dying! He knew his heart was bad. He survived two previous heart attacks. He told me he'd talked about his fear of death to Madame Jechiel—and that she made a bargain with him... She gave him a special ring."

Philip looked at her. "What kind of ring?"

"Allegedly it's from Egypt, in the shape of a beetle. Very ancient, known as the Osiris Scarab. According to what Alex told me when I asked him about it, this ring has a unique power... The scarab is apparently a symbol of immortality over there."

Philip laughed. "Utter nonsense."

"Not to Alex. She gave him the ring in exchange for a promise..." She stroked the lining of the casket.

"Which was?"

She smiled, glancing at Philip. "He refused to tell me, but he wore the ring everywhere, even to bed... when he slept, that is. That was when he began to spend long nights working in the studio, sleeping mostly during the day."

"And that was unusual?"

"Very much so. Before that, he worked maybe an hour, two hours at a time. He liked to... *brood* over his sculptures."

"What made him change?"

"I don't know, but he warned me to stay away. Kept the studio locked from the inside. After his death, I put a padlock on the studio door. I have the only key."

"This ... *person* you saw ... How did he get in?"

She paused, considering the question. "I—I don't know. All of the windows were nailed shut—and the padlock was intact."

"You have to admit, this is all pretty crazy. But I *would* like to have a talk with this Jechiel woman—to find out what kind of promise your husband made to her."

"I really appreciate your help, Mr. Dexter."

"Not help," he said, looking into her eyes, sensing her fear. "Just plain curiosity ... "

Philip's station wagon rolled to the curb in front of the Jechiel Gallery, on La Cienega a block short of Wilshire. The imposing façade, in black granite, was broken by a small window displaying a modernistic painting of the Devil astride a galloping white stallion.

Evelyn and Philip entered the gallery. In the muted glow of overhead lights, dozens of framed paintings were on display. A variety of sculptures were mounted on pedestals arranged along each wall. "Looks like we have the place to ourselves," said Philip. "Where's our mystery woman?"

At that moment, Madame Jechiel appeared from the rear of the gallery to greet them. She took Evelyn's hand. "My dear. So nice to see you again."

She was dressed entirely in black, with her graying hair pulled back in a tight bun. Her eyes were shadowed in dark make-up.

"This is Philip Dexter," Evelyn stated. "He's a writer."

"Ah, yes. I have read some of your work, Mr. Dexter. You are, one might say, an enemy of the supernatural."

Philip smiled. "You might say that."

"He wants to ask you a question," Evelyn said, glancing

at Philip.

"Regarding what?" Madame Jechiel was suddenly guarded, crossing her arms.

"Regarding Alex Court," Philip replied.

"Yes. Of course." The dark woman nodded. "I have several works of his here at the gallery. Are you interested in a purchase?"

"What I'm interested in is information. From what Mrs. Court has told me, he made you a special promise. I'd like to know what it was."

Her face tightened. "That was a personal matter between us. It doesn't concern you. Or her."

Philip put his hand up, silencing the older woman. "Mrs. Court believes her husband is alive, that she's seen him."

Madame Jechiel stared at them. "In his studio?"

Philip's tone was sharp. "How did you know *where* she saw him?"

Her reply was measured. "I know he often worked there. Perhaps his *presence* remains … "

"No *presence*," declared Philip. "She saw a real man."

"An interloper, perhaps," the old woman replied, looking away.

"That's what I thought … Now, I'm not so sure. Then there's the matter of the ring you gave him."

Jechiel looked visibly shaken. "What do *you* know about the ring?"

Philip regarded the woman, his eyes steady on hers. "Enough to make me wonder why you gave it to him."

"That's my personal business!" Madame Jechiel was getting agitated. Evelyn put a restraining hand on Philip's shoulder.

"Does your interest in the occult have something to do with the ring and the promise Court made to you?" Dexter asked, his tone softer.

Madame Jechiel looked at him, then said: "Let me warn you, Mr. Dexter, you are entering dangerous territory."

"Dangerous to whom?"

"To you both! Now go. Leave my gallery. And beware!"

"Of what?" Philip asked.

The old woman smiled.

Outside, in the station wagon, Philip tented his fingers in thought. "What was that all about?"

Evelyn sat staring from the passenger side window. Finally, she said: "I really don't know."

Philip started the car, and they drove away from Madame Jechiel's in silence. Then: "Do you have the key to your husband's studio?"

"It's in my purse."

"Okay. I want to have a look inside the place. We might find something that will shed some light on this whole weird business." He saw that she was trembling.

"I don't want to go back there," she said.

Dexter glanced over at her. "I understand, but my going in alone wouldn't do any good. You're the only one who knows the place. You know what to look for if something unusual is going on."

She looked at him. "I'm afraid, Philip."

"Don't be. I have a gun. I'll take it along." He paused. "Just in case . . . "

They reached the studio shortly after sunset. It started to rain as Evelyn keyed open the padlock and they entered. The long room was draped in shadows and dust. Her flashlight beam swept the area: Alex Court's sculptures stood along each wall, covered in white drop cloths like ghostly sentinels. The studio was ominous, with only the sound of raindrops breaking the silence.

"When you came here that night, did you get a chance to check the place out?" Philip asked, his voice loud in the quiet room.

"No," Evelyn replied. "I was barely inside the door when I saw Alex. That's when I ran."

Philip moved to a darkened corner of the studio near a dirt-grimed window. "Was it still locked from the inside?"

"Yes. I had to break the inside lock." She swept the beam toward the door. They moved deeper into the studio.

Outside, the storm had increased to a heavy downpour; rain battered the glass, intensified by a strong wind.

"Shine the light over here," said Philip.

Her flashlight illumined the area he was standing in. Philip pulled the drop cloths from a group of the works in quick succession: several were half-completed monstrosities of semi-human, semi-alien construction, sporting tortured faces and gruesomely contorted bodies. The horrendous tableaux was at once disturbing and sad. He then removed the drop cloth from a particularly massive figure. "What the Hell is *this*?"

"I—I don't know," Evelyn replied. "I—I've never seen these before."

The main figure was incredible: over fifteen feet tall and heavily-muscled, it had multiple insect-like appendages sprouting from its malformed otherworldly body. The brutal visage was little more than a nightmarish, vertically gaping maw, not unlike a vagina. The waxen skin had numerous strange textures and openings adorning it, and there were two protrusions under the twisted mouth that appeared to be crude eye sockets. Several hook-fingered hands ended the multiple arms.

"It's … horrible!" murmured Evelyn. "Like a nightmare come to life!"

"Have you ever seen your husband sculpt anything like this?" Philip asked, looking over at her.

"Never." She shuddered.

Philip circled the massive sculpture, studying the sprouted horns, the twisted genitals, the hermaphroditic physique. "Why would Court ever create such a thing?" He reached up to the clay figure's shoulder, pinching off a small portion. He rolled the small lump in his fingers. "This clay … "

"What about it?"

"It's damp. Someone's been working on this thing." He examined the sculpting tools on Court's worktable, picking up a flask of red liquid. "Looks like … blood! Why would Court need blood?"

"Let's leave, Philip!" Even in the dim light, he could see that the woman was frightened.

He ripped off a strip of cloth, dipping it into the flask. "I'm going to have this analyzed, find out what—"

A rustling sound near the opposite window drew his attention. Pulling the .45 automatic from his belt, Philip spun around to face the noise as Evelyn screamed.

In the wavering light, the manic figure of Alex Court—fierce-eyed, crouched, menacing—leaped out of the darkness. Lightning flashed outside, highlighting the lurid scene.

With a guttural cry, Court rushed at them.

"The door! Out!" Philip shouted, triggering the .45—but the bullets had no effect. Retreating from the hunched figure, Philip tipped over another heavy sculpture, trying to knock Court off-stride as they ran for the exit.

They left the building and raced for the house as the heavy rain slashed down. As they were about to reach the garage, Evelyn slipped on the wet grass, falling to the soggy earth. "We'll never make it! He's faster than we are!"

"Keep going!" Philip yelled, grabbing her arm and pulling her up.

Reaching the garage, he kicked open the side door leading into the structure and they piled into the Mercedes parked inside. Locking the doors, Evelyn jabbed in the ignition key, twisting it, but the cold engine was slow to respond. It started, then died. Again.

"He's coming!" Evelyn shrieked, beginning to panic. Philip reloaded the handgun. "Keep working it!" he shouted from the passenger's seat.

The starter whined . . . And the sliding garage door slowly opened: Court was pulling it up, trying to get in.

The car engine burst to life as Court's rancorous face filled her side window. Shattering the glass with a bony hand, he yanked the door off the car. Tossing it away, he reached up ready to smash Evelyn's skull—

"Go, go, go!" Philip yelled.

Evelyn jabbed her foot down hard on the gas pedal and the big Mercedes surged forward, smashing through the half-raised sliding door.

"You need rest," Philip said to her as they spiraled down the twisting Bel Air road toward Sunset Boulevard. "We'll drop you off at a motel. Obviously, you can't stay at the house. Then I'm going to the police."

She nodded, numb and shaking as she drove into the darkness.

Sheriff Ben Hartley leaned back in his swivel chair. He was in his late forties, balding, with a swell of gut above his belt. He squinted at Philip Dexter. "And you're telling me that the man who attacked you was Alex Court?"

"I know that face. Court was on the cover of *Time* last year. It was him. No doubt about it."

"And Mrs. Court also believes it was actually her husband?"

"That's what she believes."

The sheriff lit a filter-tip cigarette, puffing out blue smoke.

"I've been trying like hell to give up smoking," said Philip. "You're not making it any easier."

Hartley douses the cigarette. "Sorry. I shouldn't be smoking in here anyway." He shifted again in his chair. "Gotta tell you, I'm not buying your 'zombie' story. Dead men don't walk."

Philip sighed heavily, rubbing his eyes. "Agreed. But what if he *is* still alive?"

Hartley smiled. "I had my boys check the area… house, studio, garage. No walking dead man."

Dexter nodded. "It figures. He's not going to stick around waiting to be arrested for assault."

"Where is Mrs. Court now?"

"At the Seven Star. A motel in Westwood."

"I'll need to talk to her."

"Not tonight," Philip said, studying the sheriff. He rubbed his arm; he'd twisted it turning the sculpture over. "She needs to get herself together. I'll bring her by in the morning."

"Fair enough." Hartley stood. "We'll check the place out again; I can have one of my guys watch the Court residence for a few days. If he shows, we'll nab him."

The men shook hands. "Thanks, Sheriff. I've got more digging to do… "

Later that night at the motel, Philip and Evelyn discussed the police visit. She was calmer, but the harrowing events had taken an emotional toll; her voice was strained, her eyes haunted.

"I know how Alex got into the locked studio," she said. "There's a tunnel under the area—leading from the crypt to below the studio and also to the house. He came in through the trapdoor, I'm sure of it. I didn't mention it before because the only people that knew about it were Alex and myself... We used it to store wine... and in case we needed to get to the panic room under the house."

Philip rubbed his chin in thought. "Do the police know about it? Have you been down there since he 'died'?"

"No."

"And the blood ... what did you find out about that?" she asked.

"A lot. And it makes no sense."

"What do you mean?"

"According to the cops, the sample I gave them is an exact match for the blood type of that dead girl in Bel Air."

"But what was *her* blood doing in my husband's studio?"

"That's what makes no sense," Philip replied.

He sat down on the bed, lips pursed in thought. "This whole thing gets crazier by the minute. Nothing fits. Nothing is logical." He stood up. "I'm going back to talk to Hartley about the dead girl. Maybe there's a connection. Wait here for me."

The next afternoon, and Philip wasn't back yet.

In the motel, alone, Evelyn was startled by a loud tapping at the door. Nervously, she looked out of the peephole: Madame Jechiel was outside. The old woman's voice was urgent. "Hurry! Open the door!"

Jechiel entered the motel room in an agitated state. Fear clouded her dark eyes. She gripped Evelyn by both shoulders. "Thank heaven you're safe." She slumped into a chair by the bed. "I drove to your house, found it empty, checked the studio, saw the smashed garage door ... I wasn't sure you were still alive."

"How did you know where to find me?"

"I called the Sheriff's office, told them it was an emergency, and they provided this address."

Jechiel was breathing rapidly and her hands were shaking. "I can't live with it any longer ... I've got to break free ... strike back at them."

"*Them?*"

"The powers of darkness ... of evil. They've controlled me ... forced me to their bidding in exchange for success. But no longer. I *must* stop them!"

"I don't understand—"

"Then listen!" The woman gestured sharply with her hands, speaking in a heated flow of words. "When I met your husband, the thing he most feared was death. I told him about the Osiris Scarab, that by wearing it he could achieve immortality, a life beyond death ... But *only* if he agreed to serve the powers of darkness."

Evelyn stared at the old woman. "That weird figure in the studio ... "

"Yes—once the sculpture is complete, it will be able to enter our world again; its power will be *absolute* over all of humanity! And there will be more of them, oh, yes ... Entire races, waiting to take this dimension back—"

"We found a flask of blood in the studio," Evelyn said. "Is it connected to all this?"

The woman wrung her hands, her eyes gleaming. "In order that the creature may live, its body must have a certain amount of ... human blood. Alex killed the girl in Bel Air to use her blood for the sculpture."

Evelyn recoiled from the woman.

"I entered the studio to examine the figure. It is very close to completion … It lacks only eyes. Once it has sight … "

"But what can we do?" Evelyn asked.

"Court moves by night, in order to hide his diabolical efforts. Once the sun sets, he'll try to finish his awful work. We can't let that happen! We must remove the Osiris Scarab from his finger before the sun goes down. This will break the cycle and end his foul existence so that he cannot complete the work! After that we must figure out how to destroy the sculpture … " Then: "Where is Mr. Dexter?"

"With Sheriff Hartley. He'll be back soon."

"We can't wait! It's almost sundown. We must leave *now.* And pray to God we're in time … "

Dexter entered the empty motel room. On the bathroom mirror, a single scrawled word in lipstick:

STUDIO

He sprinted back to his car.

Twilight: the sun dropped closer to the horizon as Evelyn and Madame Jechiel entered the crypt. It was dim enough that they needed Evelyn's flashlight, even though a few streaks of light were still beaming in from a high window in the far wall.

"Alex wasn't in his coffin when I brought Mr. Dexter here," said Evelyn.

"Night or day?"

"It was night. I had to use the flashlight."

"That explains it. Court sleeps here by day. In a sort of trance. By night he works on the demonic sculpture."

"It's still daylight," Evelyn said. "Is he … ?"

"He's here," said the older woman. "But we must act quickly: The sun is almost down. I'm going after the ring. If something goes wrong... if I'm too late... you'll be in mortal danger. You left the mirror message for Dexter that you'll be at the studio. Wait for him there. Once I have the ring, I'll join the two of you and we'll destroy the sculpture... "

Evelyn was uncertain. "But what if—"

"Don't argue with me! Go *now*. We're almost out of time!"

Evelyn gave her the light and left the crypt.

Madame Jechiel slid the coffin from the wall, opening the lid. Court wasthere, stark and cold, eyes closed, hands by his sides. On his right index finger, the Osiris Scarab gleamed under the fading beam of her flashlight. She bent over the corpse, tugging at the ring on the dead man's finger, breath rapid, sweat beading her forehead.

At that moment, the sun dipped below the horizon and the crypt was cloaked in total darkness.

Court's eyes snapped open. His clawed hands reached for her throat. "Die, Jechiel!"

Face twisted with rage, his fingers closed around Madame Jechiel's neck. She struggled wildly trying to break his hold, but she was no match for his superhuman strength. Tossing her motionless body aside, Court stepped from the coffin.

He pressed a hand against the crypt wall and a section of the marble facing opened, revealing the dark mouth of a tunnel.

Philip's station wagon slammed to a grinding stop in front of Court's Bel Air home. Carrying a flashlight, he hurried across the moon-shadowed yard to the rear studio, finding the door unlocked. He stepped inside.

Evelyn emerged from the shadows into his ·beam. She told him about Madame Jechiel.

"Did Jechiel get the ring?"

"I don't know," she said. "Since it's dark now, I'm worried

about her."

Philip understood. "Quickly! Where's the tunnel?"

She took the flashlight and led him to the trapdoor: "Here."

Philip lifted the door, listening. "Court's in the tunnel, I think."

"Do you have your gun?"

"Doubt bullets will stop him, based on last time," said Philip. "But I do have the gun."

Evelyn grabbed a shovel from an open storage closet. "Jechiel said that we have to destroy the sculpture before Alex completes it... She said it's some kind of evil force, that if it gains entry into our world it will bring along others like it to enslave humanity. I know it sounds insane, but after all of this stuff recently... In comparison, how would it be any crazier? Who knows what'll happen if he completes it..."

Philip looked at her, considering the situation. "You're right. Crazy or not, something's going on. Even if we destroy the sculpture, though, what about Court? We can't fight him. They must *both* be destroyed. At the same time."

The sounds from the tunnel were louder now.

"He's coming!" cried Evelyn.

Philip scooped up a can of gasoline from the closet, splashing it liberally around the area. Pulling Evelyn into a shadowed corner, they crouched down behind several draped sculptures as the trapdoor pushed up and Alex Court emerged.

Court moved to a shelf, picking up a pot of fresh clay. He placed the container on a stool next to the massive sculpture as a shaft of moonlight from the window illumined the bizarre scene. He dipped his fingers into the clay and began filling in the creature's eyes. "He's almost finished!" Evelyn whispered.

Suddenly, Court dropped to his knees and began an alien chant: *"Zthy'gar... s'Yenob Absorap'th... e... ak'Xerim..."*

The figure's eyes opened as the clay twitched to life. The

creature stretched, like a great cat, while Alex Court, in rapt worship, leaned to touch his forehead to the floor.

Appearing suddenly to smell the gasoline, Court snapped his head up, looking feverishly around the room…

Philip leaped forward, brandishing the gun in one hand and his silver cigarette-lighter in the other. He thumbed it to flame and tossed it: The gasoline ignited explosively in a wave of fire as the newly animated creature thrust itself toward Philip and Evelyn.

The huge beast—half-clay, half-flesh—appeared slowed by the flames; realizing it was engulfed by the fire, the thing went berserk: snatching Alex Court in one of its monstrous appendages, it shook him fiercely. Philip and Evelyn could hear Court's breaking ribs, his snapping spine, over the roar of the blaze. Court was shrieking in agony as the beast crushed his skull between huge, clawed hands, the pulp of his cranium sizzling in the inferno as it oozed onto the thing's hands.

Philip and Evelyn ran for the outer door as the demon-creature raged, helpless to escape the flames. They saw the great creature transforming, its figure becoming deformed, its screams more pitiful as the clay popped, melting and shrinking from the intense heat, revealing the bizarre physiology of the creature's viscera.

They jumped through the door as the building erupted into a fireball…

One week later. Philip was on the phone with his publisher, Sanford Evans, again.

"That's the whole story, so obviously I can't go ahead with the original manuscript. It'll need a lot of revision. Things have changed…"

"I understand," Evans replied. "What happened after the fire?"

"Once they put it out, Sheriff Hartley found Court's bones and masses of melted clay. Looks like he was sculpting several of these 'demon' things, whatever they were ... or had tried to before he got it right ... "

"And what about the ring, Dex?"

"They found it in the pile of ashes that used to be Alex Court ... So, if I do revise the book, one last thing ... " Thunder rumbled in the distance, and Philip could see lightning on the horizon.

"Anything, Dex! You name it! Think we'll have got a real winner here. Name it! More money? Girls? A car? What?"

Philip twisted the Osiris Scarab ring slowly on his finger. "Just stop calling me 'Dex': I hate it. Like I told you, Evans—things have changed."

Tributes

GOODBYE, OLD PAL

That's what I always called him—my old pal. We were close friends for more than 60 years. I met him in Venice, California when he was 29—and now, at 91, he's gone. By his own admission, he lived a great life, did all the things he wanted to do, wrote his wonderful books and stories, was beloved around the world, won a host of awards, traveled through Europe, laughed and loved with his friends and family, and influenced millions of other writers. What more can life provide?

When I last saw him, in late March of 2012, half blind, half deaf, slow-voiced, unable to leave his bed, he was still grimly fighting death. But he knew the end was near. He gripped my hand, leaned close, and said: "Thank you for being in my life."

Of course, when we're all gone, his legendary works will remain in print. Golden apples and illustrated men and Martian chronicles and dandelion wine. They are part of us now, part of our culture. They will last.

Yes, Ray Douglas Bradbury died on June 5, 2012, but his literary children will never die.

What a man he was!

Goodbye, old pal.

God bless!

RICH

He was a close and dear friend for over half a century—one of The Group's "inner core," along with so many others lost through the years: Chuck Beaumont, Ray Bradbury, Charles Fritch, Chad Oliver, Robert Bloch—all no longer with us.

Eventually, death takes everyone; it's an unsettling, yet natural part of the lifecycle. But death is never easy, never fully integrated into our psyche: We are never quite prepared for the loss of a loved one.

And Rich was loved. By me. By his family. By his friends—indeed, by the countless thousands who read his books and stories and savored his films.

I knew at 87 he was in fragile shape—the result of several major operations; I knew he was in pain; that he could no longer really walk; that his days of swimming for exercise in his backyard pool were over; that the visits I made to his home—shared laughter, warm memories—were no longer possible. All this I sadly accepted—but the news of his death, the finality of it, the dark truth of it, hit home, struck a blow… I told myself: Rich is gone. He will always be alive in the hearts of those who cherished him. That's important; that's what counts.

And his work is still with us… the novels, the plays, the stories, the films: They will survive.

A final warm salute, then, to a master, a decent man, a good soul…

To Richard Burton Matheson: Rest easy, my friend.

The following interview was conducted in the home of Richard Matheson. It was during a visit with Mr. Matheson, in 2010, and is a part of the extensive Brock video archive of great authors, artists, and filmmakers discussing their lives, professional experiences, and friendships. Portions of some of these exclusive interviews have appeared in the JaSunni Productions feature-length documentaries TheAckerMonster Chronicles! *and* Charles Beaumont: The Twilight Zone's Magic Man.

—WFN

WHAT DREAMS MAY COME:

A Discussion with Richard Matheson and William F. Nolan. Interview by Jason V Brock

Jason V Brock: I want to ask you—a moment ago, you mentioned Jack Palance…

William F. Nolan: Yeah, Rich, let's talk a little bit about Jack Palance. How did he get chosen to play in your adaptation of *Dracula*?

Richard Matheson: Well, I believe Dan Curtis [the noted director, among other things, of *Burnt Offerings,* and the creator of *Dark Shadows*; he died of a brain tumor in 2006] chose him, and he was a very good choice.

Nolan: He had done *Dr. Jekyll and Mr. Hyde*, right? I mean for Dan, before that?

Matheson: Yeah, and very well, too, I thought.

Brock: So, did you get to know Palance?

Matheson: No, I never met him.

Left to right: *William F. Nolan, Jason V Brock, and Richard Matheson, at the Matheson home in 2010. (Courtesy Jason V Brock)*

Nolan: You weren't on the set when they were filming it then? He did a lot of that in London, didn't he? *Dracula*?

Matheson: That's right, it was all done overseas, mostly English actors.

Brock: I'm curious about something, though. Palance did *Requiem for a Heavyweight* [Rod Serling's masterful *Playhouse 90* teleplay]. Were you familiar with his work with Serling from before?

Matheson: No, not that one. I used to watch him in his action pictures, like the one with Richard Widmark…

Nolan: I believe it was *Halls of Montezuma*. Remember him as Wilson in *Shane*, as the gunfighter with the black glove? He was terrific. That's the first time I became aware of just who Jack Palance was!

Matheson: Well, the credits on *Shane* called him 'Walter Jack Palance.'

William F. Nolan and Richard Matheson, 2010. (Courtesy Jason V Brock)

Nolan: Yeah, 'Walter Jack Palance'; that was the name he was using at the time. Just like the first time that Steve McQueen was billed, in *The Blob*, he was 'Steven' … 'Steven McQueen.' You never met Palance, but you admired his work, right?

Matheson: Oh, yeah, very much so. As a matter of fact, the night I found out I had sold *The Shrinking Man* to Universal, I spent the whole night unable to sleep. And what I was doing was plotting the whole movie of *I Am Legend*, not *The Shrinking Man*, and Jack Palance was the one that I visualized as playing Robert Neville.

Brock: Oh, really? That's interesting…

Nolan: That was before you first moved back here, right? You were still living in New York then?

Matheson: We had lived out here in Gardena for quite a while. Then we moved to Long Island, in New York. Lived in Sound Beach, where I wrote *The Shrinking Man* down in the cellar.

Nolan: You were working for your brother, weren't you?

Matheson: Right. I was typing up metal address books. While we were in Sound Beach this guy named Al Manuel sold *The Shrinking Man* to Universal.

Nolan: And part of the deal was that you could write the screenplay.

Matheson: I insisted on that. At that time, the idea of selling speculative scripts was not rampant as it is today.

Brock: Fascinating. Could we go into a little bit about Rod Serling and *The Twilight Zone*?

Matheson: Sure.

Brock: How did you two meet? Was that when you started communicating with Ray Bradbury?

Matheson: No, I was in touch with Ray when I lived in Brooklyn, before I married. I read, I think it was one of his early books, *The Martian Chronicles*. So I wrote Ray a letter, you know, effusing as we all did. We were all devotees and admirers of him, and we still are—

Nolan: That's true.

Matheson: Ray wrote me back a very nice letter. I had just had the second story that I'd ever published in *Galaxy* magazine, and he said he had recently finished a story which had a similar idea. About a married couple, leaving this planet.

Nolan: "Third from the Sun," right?

Matheson: Correct. There was a scene in both our stories where the wife wonders whether they should have locked the front door, even though they were leaving the planet forever!

Brock: Sounds like something I would do! [everyone laughs]

Nolan: Ray liked your story, though, didn't he?

Matheson: Oh, yeah, yeah. And other people were starting to. I used to live with this mystery writer—Bill Gault, back when I was looking for an apartment of my own. William Campbell Gault. On the cover of *I Am Legend*, the first printing, he gave me a blurb—'This may be the most terrifying novel you've ever read.'

Nolan: That's right.

Matheson: And then on the back it read, 'You may be in at the birth of a giant.'

Nolan: 'You may be in at the birth of a giant,' and it showed a picture of Rich, you know, as a young man. Of course, Beaumont and I just leapt right on that and immediately attacked poor Rich! [to Matheson] Don't you remember how we used to tease you about that? 'We're in at the birth of a giant—and he's big. He's really big!' You know, we could never let anybody get away with that in The Group! [Nolan

The Group in the 1950s (left to right): *Charles E. Fritch, Chad Oliver, Charles Beaumont (in CB hat), Richard Matheson, Helen Beaumont (nearly out of frame). (Courtesy William F. Nolan)*

refers here to the 'Southern California Writer's Group,' as it has become known, which included Matheson, Nolan, George Clayton Johnson (*Ocean's 11*), Bradbury, Chad Oliver (*The Winds of Time*), John Tomerlin (*The Fledgling*), Charles Beaumont (*The Hunger and Other Stories*), et al.]

Matheson: [laughing] That's right, that's right. Oh, yeah, those were the good old days …

Brock: Well, you look regular-sized to me, so I guess the birth of the giant part never happened, right?

Matheson: Well, when I stand up … if I concentrate. [everyone laughs]

Brock: [to Nolan] He gets taller … and taller! [everyone laughs] Anyway, let me go back to Rod Serling and *Twilight Zone* and lead into Beaumont a little bit.

More Group madness (left to right): Chad Oliver, Charles Beaumont, Richard Matheson, William F. Nolan. (Courtesy William F. Nolan)

Nolan: Okay, but before we do, I want to clarify that point about Bradbury. When you talked to Ray, when you got the letter from him—since that was early in your career, obviously—did that kind of give you a big boost?

Matheson: Oh, of course. Of course.

Nolan: And, even though Bradbury wasn't a major writer then, he was starting to make, definitely, a name for himself.

Matheson: Exactly. He had not yet become the icon that he became.

Brock: Cool. Ray's a real sweetheart; he's a good Leo! [Bradbury was still living at the time of this interview.]

Nolan: That's right.

William F. Nolan and Richard Matheson, 2011. (Courtesy Jason V Brock)

Brock: Everybody I know is either a Pisces or a Leo. [Nolan, Matheson, and Brock are all Pisces.]

Matheson: Well, I've known several developed Leos and they're good. Good people.

Brock: Developed Pisces are good, too.

Matheson: Right. I'm a developed Pisces. I mean, we've known a number of couples where the Taurus/Pisces combination [Matheson's wife is a Taurus] was reversed and the woman was the Pisces and the man was the Taurus. That didn't work out at all; in several of those cases, the woman was alcoholic…

Brock: Addiction is common in Pisces.

Matheson: Yeah.

Nolan: Oh, that's ridiculous! Astrology is nonsense!

Brock: Declares the man who believes aliens built the pyramids! [laughs] Anyway ... So, let me ask you, Rich—

Matheson: You know, my whole family was full of alcoholics.

Brock: Wow.

Matheson: There's no one left, though. That's why I was finally able to write my play about my family—because there's nobody left to hurt.

Nolan: [to Matheson] None of your children became addicted to anything—

Matheson: Writing! [everyone laughs]

Nolan: It's a curse, Rich!

Matheson: I figure that's the only reason I don't drink heavily is because I get it all out in my writing—

Nolan: Hemingway said that the best psychiatrist in the world is a sheet of white bond paper rolled into your typewriter.

Brock: I think that writing can be addictive, for sure. And music, too.

Matheson: I remember the best definition of a writer I ever heard was 'a writer is someone who cannot not write.'

Nolan: That's true. We're driven to it. I didn't pick writing out, writing picked me. Because you start at the age of eight or nine or ten, and from then on you write and you don't think about ever being a professional.

Ruth and Richard Matheson in the 1950s. (Courtesy William F. Nolan)

Brock: I kind of get hooked on revision. I like to revise what I've written. I'm a chronic reviser. I like to revise and revise and revise.

Matheson: Oh, well, I do that, too.

Nolan [to Matheson]: When you were doing all those short stories, didn't you do several drafts of each story before you submission?

Matheson: Well, I did when Tony Boucher or J. Francis McComas [editors of *The Magazine of Fantasy and Science Fiction*] had suggestions; I would make a lot of revisions. And it was always helpful. Almost always... And if it wasn't helpful, I didn't agree with it. Now, if publishers buy it, they print it, just the way I wrote it.

Brock: With novels you have to plot things out more carefully;

I like to plot everything out in advance, then leave myself a little room for wiggle, so that if I run into a thing I didn't think about with the original structure, I can easily remedy the issue. There seems to be a preference now for novels, don't you think, versus short fiction?

Matheson: Well, short fiction is done.

Nolan: Short story collections don't do nearly as well as novels.

Matheson: No, they don't.

Nolan: And the market for short stories is almost nil. I was telling him [motions to Brock] that he's trying to break in now in a soft market. When you and I broke in, there were thirty or forty well-paying magazines we could sell to. But not anymore.

Matheson: That's originally why I went into science fiction. I knew nothing about it when I sold "Born of Man and Woman." Everybody said, 'Hey, that's science fiction. That's a mutation story.' I said, 'What's science fiction?'

Nolan: So you thought, 'What the hell, it's a good market: I'll go for it.'

Matheson: Exactly. There were so many science fiction magazines I thought, 'Well, okay, I better learn.' I went out and gathered all these anthologies and read them.

Brock: So *Shrinking Man* brought you out here. Is that what brought you to the attention of Rod Serling? Is that how you started working with Rod on *Twilight Zone*?

Left to Right: William F. Nolan, Richard Matheson, Ruth Matheson at the Matheson home in 2011. (Courtesy Jason V Brock)

Matheson: Well, in the beginning Rod wanted to hire more writers from the field.

Brock: Because he was overcommitted.

Matheson: Right. He tried all the top writers in the field, and he found out that it didn't work because *Twilight Zone* had a specific structure to it, and if you couldn't do that structure, that was it. And most of those stories are, you know, different; as I have been quoted, the stories—the great classics at least—are not easy to write.

Most of the writers he tried to use in the beginning would do something like create a story where the main character would meet somebody on a train, and that character would tell you a story like, 'My Uncle Ferdinand had a horrible experience . . . '

Then they'll tell you all about Uncle Ferdinand, and the last line is, 'There, in the giant moth, was Uncle Ferdinand's face.' That's not a *Twilight Zone*. So Chuck [Beaumont] and I were already in the field; plus we knew how to adapt our work quickly, and we understood the structure: You give them a teaser that makes their interest perk up, and you have a first act. Then, you have like a cliffhanger at the end of the first act; finally, you move to the end, and hopefully, a surprise ending with the climax.

Brock: Did you meet Beaumont then, or did you know him previously?

Matheson: No, no. I met him when I first came to California in 1951.

Brock: How did that happen?

Matheson: I guess I must've written to him or something. He and Helen came to see me when I lived in a room on Wilshire Boulevard. I remember them coming to see me, and then I went to see them in their apartment later.

Nolan: Up on Friar, right? In that second story?

Matheson: I don't know whether it was that one. It may have been a different apartment.

Nolan: You weren't married to Ruth then when you first met Chuck, were you?

Matheson: No. Chris [Beaumont] was a six-month-old baby in his crib, I remember. I came out in '51 and then in '53, as I mentioned, when we were living in Gardena, things weren't going well so I decided to take the job with my brother... That's when we moved back east.

Brock: Because your family was back there.

Matheson: Yeah. My brother offered to give me a job, so I went back and found out that I didn't really want to live there, and I wrote *The Shrinking Man*.

Nolan: Didn't you say at the time that if *The Shrinking Man* doesn't sell, 'I'm through with writing. I'm going to go into business.' Wasn't that true?

Matheson: Well, my brother wanted me to become his partner…

Brock: What did he have again? A printing firm or something?

Matheson: It was a direct mail place where magazines, like *Disney Magazine* and *Red Cross Magazine*, would all have to buy the printed names and addresses that are to be sent out each month. You would type them up on this address-ograph machine and it came out in little plates, and then he would sell these plates to whatever magazine.

Nolan: So you typed the addresses up on the machine for a while then, huh? The point I'm trying to make is that you took a final shot with *The Shrinking Man*, and said, correct me if I'm wrong, that 'If this doesn't go, I'm going to give up writing and join my brother.'

Matheson: Well, that may have been an empty threat on my part, too! [everyone laughs] I mean, I can't believe now that, writing being so important to me, I would really have given it up entirely. I probably would've become his partner, but if I had, I would probably be secretly writing little short stories when nobody was looking…

Brock: Like Kafka. Kafka is excellent.

Matheson: [smiles] Yeah, and weird. I mean, the guy wakes up and he's a giant cockroach, for God's sake! I might have realized that I had achieved something if I saw some review in Europe where they compared me to Kafka. I'd have thought 'Ah, I've made it at last!'

Brock: I like Borges, too.

Matheson: Luis Borges, I like him as well.

Nolan: How about the one that Chuck made into a film, *The Circus of Doctor Lao*. That's a wonderful book—

Matheson: Yes, by Charles Finney.

Brock: So when Chuck and Helen came over to your place, how long before you became such close friends? Did that develop from there or did it come later? He got hired first [for *The Twilight Zone*], I guess, right? Or did you get hired at the same time?

Matheson: This was pre-*Twilight Zone*. This was several years before; we're talking '51 now. *Twilight Zone* was much later.

Nolan: That was in '57, '58.

Brock: So you and Chuck were very close friends by the time *Twilight Zone* came along…

Nolan: You'd been friends for years by then.

Matheson: Sure, sure. When we had our kids we were almost the same age. Then we met you [motions to Nolan], and we all got along. It just went on from there. It developed into a real lifelong friendship between us.

Nolan: Now, the way that *Twilight Zone* happened, and again, Rich can correct me if I'm wrong on this, weren't you and Chuck called to a sort of free screening with a lot of other writers—

Matheson: That's right.

Nolan: Rod set that up. A screening of the pilot; he invited Matheson and Beaumont and a lot of other people, and the only two that emerged were you and Chuck that he wanted to use as writers. The others didn't understand how to do a *Twilight Zone*.

Matheson: Correct. At that point, we were the only two. Later on, he used some other writers also, like Earl Hamner (*The Waltons*), George Johnson, people like that.

Nolan: God, if you leave the 'Clayton' out around George, you're finished! [Playfully imitating Johnson's voice] 'My name is George Clayton Johnson.'

Brock: I love the way, when he signs his name, he'll write a little copyright thing—

Nolan: I joke with him about that. I say, 'George, make sure nobody steals your name, right?' And he says, 'Yes! I must guard against all those other plain George Johnsons out there!' No, we never let anybody get away with anything in The

Group. The minute something like that happened, all of us would descend on that person and rip them apart.

Matheson: I avoided the trips to the beach for that reason! That was bad news. 'We're taking you to purgatory tonight.' [Matheson refers here to a ritual in The Group where bad news would be heaped upon an offending member of the circle by way of a long verbal berating, known figuratively as 'being taken to the beach.']

Nolan: We'd come in and we'd point to somebody and say, 'We're taking you to the beach tonight!' and, boy, that person would just wilt because it was like two hours of interrogation. That was death!

Brock: Now, you got along with Rod pretty well? Was he easy to work with?

Matheson: Oh, definitely. He was as nice as could be. I mean, being a writer himself, he appreciated good writing and never changed it. I don't recall one word of my scripts ever being changed except by some actress in an episode with Keenan Wynn.

Nolan: See, the thing about Rod Serling and *Twilight Zone*, as related to Chuck and Rich, is that this is one of the few times, if not the only time, that their scripts were shot exactly as they wrote them without changing, without rewriting, without cutting. Rod respected both of them so much that he left their scripts alone—

Matheson: That's right.
Brock: Now, what about you, Chuck, and your work habits?

You guys were quite different as individuals, and also very different kinds of writers…

Matheson: Not in script form, though. Like the thing we did on *Burn, Witch, Burn*.

Brock: For Roger Corman? [Corman is a well-respected director and producer, whose credits include several cinematic Edgar Allan Poe adaptations.]

Matheson: Right. Not the original name of it, you know: it was *Conjure Wife*.

Nolan: By Fritz Leiber.

Matheson: [nods affirmatively] I wrote the first half, Chuck wrote the second half. Then we each looked at it and made some corrections. But our script writing was very similar. We started with Westerns and everything, with things like *Wanted Dead or Alive*. Now, when we were working on those together, Chuck would go out and have the meetings and set up the thing, and I would sit home and write it with him.

I was lazy. I said, 'I'll do the first draft. You go out and take the meetings.' And then all these producers became convinced I was this syphilitic lost soul out in the sticks who couldn't write well at all!

Nolan: There came a day when you decided, 'Nuts to this! I'm going to stop this collaboration with Beaumont because I'm being perceived as some kind of lump sitting home, writing, while the great Beaumont goes out and all the selling.' So they quit writing together at that point. I mean, isn't that right, Rich?

Matheson: Yeah. There was this one producer—William something—but he was convinced that I didn't know how to write. I was watching his program one night—he had a talk show on cable and he was interviewing [producer] George Eckstein. And he was saying to him, 'You know, this whole idea that it's Steven Spielberg's *Duel* is ridiculous. It should really be . . . ' and I thought, 'Ah-ha! At last I get credit!' when he says, 'called George Eckstein's *Duel*.'

Brock: Oh, God! [everyone laughs]

Matheson: I said, 'The hell with it . . . '

Nolan: Rich always says that he and Spielberg 'started together' because *Duel* was the first major work that Spielberg directed.

Brock: Spielberg had done some work with Rod on the *Night Gallery* pilot film, right? I think that was his first big thing.

Matheson: *Eyes* with Joan Crawford, I think. That was her last thing, as I recall. That was Spielberg's, like, very first non-student thing.

Brock: I assume you guys met [meaning Spielberg and Matheson]. Did you meet through Rod?

Matheson: Actually, I never met Steve until I went out to watch him shoot at this coffee shop on the old Ridge Route. I thought, 'What did they do? They're shutting down, or they're letting it run as a business while they're shooting this thing?' I didn't realize that everybody there was an actor, 'cause they were so realistic.

Brock: Wow, interesting. What's he like? He's pretty nice, I bet.

Matheson: Oh, he's always been very nice to me.

Brock: *Duel* was incredible. I loved Dennis Weaver in it. Stephen King did a sequel to it, right? With Joe Hill? In that tribute anthology [*He Is Legend*].

Nolan: Right, it's about a motorcycle gang that's terrorized by a truck. It's not the same truck driver, though.

Brock: I see. Rich, what did you think of the Lily Tomlin *Shrinking Woman* movie?

Matheson: If it had been really funny I would not have minded, but it was not funny. I mean, I don't care if they want to make a satire out of something I've written. Apparently, *The Simpsons* did some great satires of "Nightmare at 20,000 Feet." "Nightmare at 6½ Feet" or something.

Brock: What did you think about that whole, not to delve into this, but you know, the whole *Twilight Zone* thing got kind of topsy-turvy when the movie came out and all that happened with Vic Morrow? [Morrow and two children were accidentally killed on the set.] Did you like *Twilight Zone: The Movie* in general?

Matheson: I don't usually like anthology movies. The only movie I ever saw that I thought worked was the British one…

Nolan: *Dead of Night*, you're talking about *Dead of Night*, aren't you?

Matheson: *Dead of Night*, yeah. As a matter of fact, Dan [Curtis] used that title, I think.

Nolan: He did. In a series that never sold.

Matheson: I didn't think *Twilight Zone* really worked as a film. It didn't translate. I did the script for a lot of it. It was much harder-edged, initially, for example, in the piece based on George's story ["Kick the Can"]. I thought Joe Dante did a nice job on the other one, though.

Brock: That's the Jerome Bixby segment ["It's a Good Life"].

Matheson: Yeah, well there's a guy who wrote music [meaning Bixby].

Brock: Did he?

Matheson: Oh, yeah, orchestrated and everything.

Brock: Oh, I didn't know that about him.

Matheson: Yeah, he and I spoke on the phone.

Brock: Fascinating. What was his sign?

Matheson: That I don't know.

Brock: That'd be interesting to know … maybe he's a Pisces.

Matheson: Could be. At that time I wasn't into those things so much.

Brock: Music runs in both of our families. [Brock is a guitarist; Matheson is a composer/pianist.] Pisceans are known for their musicality… R. C. [Matheson] is a drummer right?

Matheson: Oh, he's a marvelous drummer. Richard [referring to his son] was at some party recently where he was playing the drums for somebody, and this guy who was in the business asked him to sit in with his other group, a professional group. R. C. had a house in Malibu, and he had this room down below soundproofed, and you couldn't hear anything from the outside; in fact, he was pounding away on his drums, and it kept getting hotter and hotter, to the point he thinks 'I'm really getting hot here!' and it turned out that the Malibu fire was right outside!

Nolan: It got hot alright: It burned the whole house down! He lost the house.

Brock: [surprised laugh] That's terrible! That's kind of a funny story, but it's horrible…

Nolan: 'I'm getting hot, jeez!' And the damn fire was right outside! He rebuilt on the same lot though, didn't he Rich?
Matheson: Right. This contractor who's done a lot of work on our house, then was working on his house, knocked on the door and said, 'Richard, do you know there's a fire outside?' Yeah, he rebuilt there.

Brock: That's pretty crazy… So, getting back to the topic, you and Chuck obviously worked well together. Did you work in the same office?

Matheson: No, nobody worked in offices. I guess when I did

The Shrinking Man [a reference to writing the script], I did work in an office at Universal, but with *Twilight Zone*, we just worked at home.

Nolan: I want to ask something about Rod Serling. Rich, were you aware that Rod smoked three or four packs a day, that he always had a cigarette in his hand?

Matheson: Well I knew that his father had died at the age of fifty, and probably from the same reason. And he … the smoking certainly didn't help any, but Rod was under stress all the time. I remember once we went to his house because he had this film society, where each person would choose two films that they wanted to look at, and then they'd rent it and show it on a projector. That night they were showing *The Incredible Shrinking Man*. Rod came home, late, and the first thing he said to Carol was, 'I've had a bitch of a day.'

Nolan: A bitch of a day, huh?

Matheson: Yeah, and he had. You know *Twilight Zone* at least was some sort of satisfaction to him. *Night Gallery*, was no satisfaction at all.

Brock: Now you also worked on *Night Gallery* …

Matheson: Correct … that was when one of the producers wasn't crazy about what I did.

Brock: Jack Laird.

Matheson: [nods] He didn't care for Rod's work, either.

Brock: You wrote two *Night Gallery* episodes didn't you?

Matheson: Right, I wrote one which featured John Carradine, who had done a marvelous *Lawman*. At the time, I felt more satisfaction out of *Lawman* than I did at *Twilight Zone*.

Nolan: Well you won an award for *Lawman*.

Brock: You know, we talk about The Group; I don't want to interrupt, but I do want to put this in before we forget: With regard to Group relationships—Guess who wrote a lot of *Lawman* episodes? John Tomerlin.

Matheson: Tomerlin was writing a lot of *Lawman* episodes at that time, yes.

Brock: Did you know John very well back then? Were you guys social?

Matheson: Oh sure, all the time. John and Wilma [Tomerlin's wife] were always over; we would usually go to Beaumont's house or they would come to ours. John became a real car expert. Bill [Nolan] and Chuck as well.

Brock: You didn't get into cars … well you got into them, but you didn't … [everyone laughs]

Matheson: What's the dedication of that first book, Bill?

Nolan: [reciting] It was something like 'To Wilma Tomerlin, for beauty beyond the call of duty, and to Richard Matheson, who knows nothing about cars and could not care less—'

Matheson: 'Whose profound misunderstanding of motor sports … '

Nolan: Oh that's right, that's it, you've got it: 'Whose profound misunderstanding of cars and motor sports,' that's right yeah… [to Brock] Chuck and I dedicated a book to Rich [*The Omnibus of Speed*]. Yes, that's right: 'profound misunderstanding.' No, Rich was never interested in the sports car scene the way Tomerlin, Beaumont, and I were. We would go out to these road races on weekends, and Rich would say 'Good luck, I'm staying home.'

Matheson: I think if I'd gotten into one of those cars I probably would've killed myself in the first race! [everyone laughs]

Brock: Back on topic here, I recently talked to Ray [Bradbury] a little about The *Twilight Zone*—

Matheson: He was not too happy with Rod.

Brock: Well, he talked a little bit about it because I sense he liked Rod… They were friends I know for a while. But Ray felt betrayed when the electric grandmother story [Bradbury's adaptation of his "I Sing the Body Electric"] was cut, because he was a real influence on Rod—

Matheson: Sure. On everybody!

Brock: On everybody, exactly. Bradbury was a titan, of course. [pause] Still, what do you think? Do you think he was too hard on Rod, or do you think that he was right in his assessment?

Matheson: Well, I've had that done to me. I remember once, I wrote a pilot script for a war series [*Combat!*] with Vic Morrow, and they sent me a copy of the script and I thought, 'Now they've sent me the wrong one; this must be by somebody else, this is not mine.' Everything was different—technical, panorama, the whole different color pages. They changed all of it. I told them, fairly, I thought, that I wasn't happy about it. As a matter of fact, I think that's where I invented my pen name: Logan Swanson—

Brock: Oh, right.

Matheson: Which is, loosely, my mother's maiden name. Years later I spoke to the guy who had produced *Combat!*. I said, 'Why did you do that?' and he said, 'We didn't change anything.' They're living in this dream world. 'We don't change anything.' That's true: They change *everything!*

Brock: Wow …

Matheson: I've written a lot, and I've decided that writers are like the pariahs of the business—but they can't live without us. Billy Wilder, I recall, once walked into a producer's office, threw down a script of completely blank pages, and said: 'Okay. Put your 'touch' on this … '

Brock: [laughs] So, when Bradbury and Serling stopped working together, was that a hard thing for Rod?

Matheson: Well, sure. There were a number of Ray's stories that could have been used. He was very successful. I mean, Ray did his own series, years later, up in Canada.

Brock: Did you like *The Ray Bradbury Theater*? I enjoyed it; I thought it had some good things. And I loved Ray's adaptation of *Something Wicked This Way Comes.*

Matheson: Sure, I have *Ray Bradbury Theater* on DVDs around here somewhere. As for *Something Wicked*, it has an aura, a marvelous feeling of small town America … leaves blowing in October, and all the things that Ray wrote about are in that movie. I liked it a lot, but it didn't make a dime; it just … died.

Brock: Too bad. It's a beautiful little film, I think. So how do you feel about your adaptation of *The Martian Chronicles*?

Matheson: Truthfully, I wasn't happy with it, and neither was Ray. The only one we both liked was the one where the Martian winds up in the church. He hid out from a mob in this church. And this preacher, this minister is there, and the dream of his life was that he could meet Jesus and talk to him, so he meets this Martian, and starts believing he might be Jesus. The Martian says: 'I'm not who you think I am.' But the priest is so bound to this idea that he will not let go, and as long as he won't let go of the guy, the Martian can't leave, even though it gives him physical agony to continue in a different form. It was done really well.

Nolan: That one was well done. It's an excellent story, but somehow the whole miniseries was just too … ponderous.

Matheson: It was. The only other scene I felt came through was the one where Rock Hudson meets the Martian and they realize that they are centuries apart.

Nolan: That was a good story in the book too. Now, I have another important question I want to ask; I'm going to ask you the same question I asked Bradbury, Rich: If Chuck Beaumont were alive today, where do you think he'd be, in relation to writing?

Matheson: Oh, I believe he would've written more and more important things all the time. [pauses] I mean the subject matter he wrote about was quite important, I think.

Nolan: Do you think he would have veered away from science fiction and fantasy and into more mainstream writing?

Matheson: Absolutely. I don't think he was dedicated to either one of those. Do you know what sign Chuck was? I don't recall.

Brock: Capricorn. January second.

Matheson: Well he—it's a cruel thing to say about Capricorn, but it's like a 'sellout' sign.

Brock: Interesting. A sellout sign?

Matheson: What I mean is that, too many times, Chuck sold out his ability because he needed to make money. When he was on his own, he wrote as he would, as he wished. *Playboy* stuff, like "Black Country," I mean, they were marvelous! I remember the night he read it to us in his apartment...

Nolan: Right. I did a reading of it on tape, myself. But let me tell you something about "Black Country" that fits right into what you just said, Rich.

When Chuck first wrote "Black Country," he was living on the second floor up on Friar Street, in that little apartment up there, and one night we were sitting together on the floor I remember, I was sitting on the floor cross-legged, and he had just finished the first draft of "Black Country," and he set up the funeral for Spoof Collins, the black trumpeter, on Mars. And I said, 'Chuck, this is too good for Mars! You don't need to try to turn it into a genre science fiction story. You should just do a straight story of a black trumpeter that dies of cancer at the height of his fame.' And he took my word and the reason "Black Country" is not science fiction is because I told him to drop the Martian opening. Otherwise it would have been just another science fiction tale.

Matheson: Oh, it's a wonderful story. Chuck had a superb facility with words.

Nolan: He loved the English language, didn't he?

Matheson: Exactly, that's why I'm so impressed with Richard [referring again to R. C. Matheson]—he does the same thing. He uses adjectives and descriptions so well, even in his scripts. He's the one that taught me that, it doesn't hurt to do some vivid description in a script. I used to write them just barebones.

Nolan: Well we all did, certainly. We let the director put the imagery in …

Matheson: I said to Richard, 'Why do that? Because the director will do it on their own anyway,' and he said, 'You don't do it for the director; you do it for the people who you're hoping to sell to.'

Nolan: Yes, it makes it more readable, that's for sure.

Matheson: Sure. More entertaining.

Brock: That's interesting. So you think Chuck would have veered more and more into … ?

Matheson: Oh, I think he would have become a very important writer. I read another collection of his stories [*A Touch of the Creature*], and it had stories in there I never knew he'd written, with elements in them that I never knew he was even thinking about. It has only one fantasy story in it, at the beginning. All the rest are straight pieces. It's a whole other side of Beaumont. Fascinating, just fascinating. That gives credence to the idea that he would've gone more and more into that area.

Brock: How did you feel about Chuck's passing? How did that impact you?

Matheson: [pauses] You know, it was like a vivid element in our life was just … taken away. And unfairly.

Nolan: Exactly. That's perfect. That's exactly how it felt.

Matheson: I mean, he provided so much energy. He'd introduce you to new things, new people. I remember him introducing me to Chico Hamilton's Quintet—

Nolan: Yep. I still have those LP records!

Matheson: And he had a great taste for art; he would have special paintings and sketches that he would buy when he went on a trip … He was bright and, like I said, had such vivid use of language. And he was funny, very funny. I still miss him.

Nolan: Very dynamic, very alive; always moving. Always on the go.

Matheson: Whenever he called he would say 'Mathewson, it is I.' [smiles]

Nolan: That's right! Bradbury got that started; it was Ray that used to call you Mathewson all the time. For years. And you would say to him, 'Ray, my name is *Matheson*.' And he would say 'Of course, Mathewson! Right, your name is Matheson.

Of course it is.' And, from then on, it would be right back to Mathewson!

You got really pretty annoyed after a while because you'd told Bradbury about ten times, 'Matheson, my name is Matheson!' So of course, Beaumont being Beaumont, he immediately picked up on the Mathewson thing, and would call you on the phone [imitating Beaumont]: 'This is Beaumarg, calling Mathewson.' Or 'Charles Bumar looking for Dick Mathewson.' You remember Chuck had all those crazy names for himself? 'Bumall here ... '

Matheson: We were always joking around back then ... Someone just sent me something I had written—little sheets of a note to Chuck—where I'd said, 'I will never finish the play with you. I will not write or collaborate with you on any scripts anymore. I will not see you any longer. I am going to have a brain operation, so I don't even think about you!' and on and on. Horrible! [laughs] At the bottom of the letter, I had handwritten: 'See you soon. Love, Dick'

Nolan: 'Love, Dick.' [laughs] Yeah, everything was 'Dick Matheson' for years. It was always 'Dick' this and 'Dick' that, and one day—

Matheson: Yeah, most of my family called me that ...

Nolan: [to Brock] I remember one day Dennis Etchison called Rich 'Dick,' and Rich says: 'Don't call me Dick! Nobody calls me Dick but Bill Nolan, and he can do it 'cause I've known him so long ... '

Matheson: That's right. But even you call me Rich, now.

Brock: What prompted the change in name?

Matheson: Well, as soon as I met Ruth in 1951 she called me Rich. No one had ever called me that before, so that's what everybody calls me these days.

Brock: So, with relation to Chuck, is there a favorite Beaumont piece of yours?

Matheson: Well "Black Country" is wonderful …

Nolan: I would agree that's probably Chuck's best story, overall.

Matheson: *The Intruder* is an excellent novel. I remember when he went down South to research it, and then when you all did the film with Roger [Corman].

Nolan: William Shatner deserved an Academy Award nomination for that role [Shatner portrayed white supremacist Adam Cramer]. He's never been better. Never.

Matheson: I agree. Isn't that the picture where he slapped you so hard [references Nolan]?

Nolan: That's the one. Shatner knocked me completely out of frame! We did the rehearsal and he said 'Now don't worry Bill, I'll pull my punch just before it hits your neck' and I said 'Okay … because you know I don't want to really get hit.' And he said, 'Don't worry. I'm a professional. I know how to do this.' And he smiles, very friendly.

So the time comes for the actual scene, and I said, 'What we gonna do now?' and I was all upset and he said, 'Shut up!' and he whacks me across the neck; he hit me so hard I went completely out of the frame … When you see me come back in, I'm all flushed and really pissed off, 'cause I didn't want to be hit. [everyone laughs] Afterwards he came up to me and said, 'Look, Bill, I'm sorry I hit you but we needed it for the realism.'

I'll tell one more story about Shatner you'll find amusing: We're sitting in this café in Sikeston, Missouri, and they had gelled all the windows. You know, these big gelled curtains that they drop … Anyway, the heat was incredible. I'm sweating like a pig: Sweat is rolling down my face, sweat is under my hat, sweat is under my arms. So Shatner's sitting there in a white linen suit, not a bead of sweat on him.

I said, 'My God, Shatner! How come you're not sweating?' And he just smiles and says, 'Simple. In this movie your character sweats. He's a lowlife … My character is the mastermind—he's not supposed to sweat.' So that was his answer: He could control the sweat on his body. How many actors can do that? [everyone laughs]

Matheson: Long before he did any of my *Twilight Zone*s and *Star Trek*, I used to, when I lived in Brooklyn, watch him on television. I'd go out of my way to watch him because I thought he was so good …

Brock: He did Broadway too quite a bit, right?

Nolan: That's right; I saw him in *Suzie Wong* on Broadway.

Matheson: I actually saw him in that, too: *The World of Suzie Wong*.

Brock: Getting back to The *Twilight Zone*, when the series ended, how did you feel about that? Were you worried about income, about getting more work?

Matheson: [pauses] No, not really. I was doing *Lawman*; then

I went into Movies of the Week. I seem to have a penchant for doing 'women in jeopardy' pictures, which was the big thing back then.

Brock: Is that when you started working with Dan Curtis? Or was that later?

Matheson: No, that was later. When I met Dan, he was going to do *The Night Stalker*. I was unpleasant to him, because he'd made a very low offer to option one of my novels. But, rather than murder me, luckily he accepted me! [laughs] Then I wrote the Stalker script. When I went to check on the production, we were on a trip with the family, and we stopped in Las Vegas, where they were shooting *Night Stalker*; I looked at the script and it was full of these technical panorama things where every other page was a different color, and I thought 'Oh my God! They've done it to me again!' and I left in a fury.

Darren McGavin for years thought I was an idiot because I did that. I finally made peace with Dan and explained the whole situation. But then when I saw the movie, I realized they hadn't changed that much of my script. It was very well done. That's when I told Bill to join Curtis and myself.

Nolan: [to Matheson] You know Rich, I think we were Dan's favorite writers. I worked on more than fifteen projects with him, and you wrote a lot for him as well. He kept coming back to us because we all worked so well together.

Matheson: That's true. We made him laugh. That was the key. He could be quite fierce, but always had an excellent sense of humor. It was a fine time. We all miss Dan.

Made in the USA
Middletown, DE
08 February 2020